Praise for Pamela Britton

"Britton creates another fast-moving, heartrending romance where love triumphs, even in adverse conditions."
—*RT Book Reviews* on *Slow Burn*

"This new installment in Britton's NASCAR series is the best yet. It not only brings alive the sport but also the emotional roller coaster of those who have a loved one suffering from cancer. The story is heart-achingly real but also wonderfully hopeful. It's an incredible read."
—*RT Book Reviews* on *Total Control*

"*To the Limit* is a smooth read... It's a well-written racing story with romance, fun and excitement!"
— Joyfully Reviewed

Praise for Dorien Kelly

"Complex characters facing multiple challenges make this novel a page-turner."
—*RT Book Reviews* on *Over the Wall*

"Warmly appealing thanks to its assured prose and deft characterizations."
—*Publishers Weekly* on *Hot Nights in Ballymuir*

"[The hero] is fabulous—if he's not the perfect male, he's close—and Kelly makes good use of attraction between the characters...as they draw closer in this singularly intense romance."
—*RT Book Reviews* on *The Littlest Matchmaker*

PAMELA BRITTON

Before the glitz and glamour of NASCAR, Pamela wrote books that were frequently voted the best of the best by *The Detroit Free Press*, Barnes & Noble (two years in a row) and *RT Book Reviews*. She's won numerous writing awards, including a National Reader's Choice Award, and a nomination for Romance Writers of America's Golden Heart.

When not following the race circuit, Pamela writes full-time from her ranch in Northern California, where she lives with her husband, daughter and, at last count, twenty-one four-legged friends. Pamela's always happy to hear from readers. You can reach her through her website, www.pamelabritton.com, or via regular mail at: P.O. Box 804, Cottonwood, CA 96022.

DORIEN KELLY

lives in Michigan with one or more of her three children, two westies and a special-needs coonhound named Bubba. When she's not writing, she's simply avoiding her writing deadlines. Or possibly out having fun....

NASCAR®

This Time, Forever

Pamela Britton 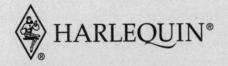 Dorien Kelly

HARLEQUIN®

TORONTO • NEW YORK • LONDON
AMSTERDAM • PARIS • SYDNEY • HAMBURG
STOCKHOLM • ATHENS • TOKYO • MILAN • MADRID
PRAGUE • WARSAW • BUDAPEST • AUCKLAND

ISBN-13: 978-0-373-18541-2

THIS TIME, FOREVER

Copyright © 2010 by Harlequin Books S.A.

The publisher acknowledges the
copyright holders of the individual works
as follows:

Recycling programs
for this product may
not exist in your area.

OVER THE TOP
Copyright © 2010 by Harlequin Books S.A.
Pamela Britton is acknowledged as the author of "Over the Top."

TALK TO ME
Copyright © 2010 by Harlequin Books S.A.
Dorien Kelly is acknowledged as the author of "Talk to Me."

NASCAR® and the NASCAR Library Collection® are registered
trademarks of the National Association for Stock Car Auto Racing, Inc.

CONTENTS

An excerpt from Hilton Branch's prison journal...

You can always count on Maeve. I don't know how she managed it, what she had to say to get Penny to visit, but somehow she did. I couldn't explain everything in a letter. Who knows who is reading my mail in this godforsaken place?

So she came here, my princess, to this place that stinks of misery. And she looked at me with pity instead of the admiration my little girl always had for her daddy. It was a bitter pill.

Far more bitter, though, was my news for her.

She cried, my Penny. And hates me a little more for the fresh evidence of my disloyalty.

I had to explain, too, about the money I'd put in Fred Clifton's hands for safekeeping for Rose and her girls. The look of betrayal in Penny's eyes killed me. Nearly everything she had was tied up in my company's stock, and when it collapsed, she was nearly bankrupt, just like her mother and her brothers. To learn that I'd made provisions for a second family when I hadn't protected my first one...

Never have I felt more a failure as a man. Rose would hate me, too, if she knew.

But she may hate me already for my desertion, never knowing that I did it to protect her.

I can almost live with that, as long as she's safe—she, and her Amelia and our Lily.

I've run out of options. I talked to the prison shrink, the only person in this place I can trust. I laid out the threats and asked her—begged her—to go to the police with them. Not for me, but for my loved ones. My children and Rose.

Dr. Danforth didn't say it in so many words, but the message was clear—my credibility is in question. The police know that I've lied to them before and don't trust me now.

I'd lie for attention, they say. Because I need to feel important.

Damn them—in former days, they would have been jumping when I snapped my fingers. Now lives—good lives, worthy lives, precious lives—are at stake, and all I hear about are jurisdictional issues. That it will take time.

I don't have time. My children don't have time. Saunders had men stake me out in the exercise yard. They made it clear that they could take my life between one heartbeat and the next.

He doesn't understand that my own life means nothing to me now.

But my children's lives mean everything.

I cannot wait for the authorities to act. And so I begged my daughter to help Rose and her daughters. In the end, the mother in Penny won out—she has agreed to look for Rose and Lily and Amelia and help me keep them safe. She will talk to her brothers, too, and warn them.

She didn't promise to return to visit, however. Seeing her frigid contempt was a blow. Maeve was right when she told me that, in my search for wealth and power, I sacrificed the real treasure that was my children's love.

I did better with Lily, in our brief time together, but that is small comfort now.

All I can do is sit back and hope.

Over the Top

Pamela Britton

For all my coffee shop pals…
you know who you are. You guys make my days brighter!

$$141$$
$$292$$
$$\overline{4.33}$$
$$182$$
$$\overline{41.5}$$

CHAPTER ONE

"HE's here."

Marley Sizemore glanced up from the document she'd been studying and resisted the urge to shake her head. There was no need to ask who *he* was. Linc Shepherd, Double S Racing's newest driver was slated to arrive today, and she knew for a fact that Emma-Lee Dalton was one of his biggest fans, something her new boyfriend, Holt Forrester, seemed to put up with.

"Well then, what are you doing up here?" Marley teased. "You should be downstairs, asking for an autograph."

Emma-Lee looked like a cat who'd just seen the world's biggest mouse. "Oh. Do you think he'd mind? I've always wanted to get his autograph. I even have one of his die-cast cars at home; the first car he drove. The one he won the NASCAR Sprint Cup Series championship in. Shoot. I should have brought it with me today."

Marley couldn't keep herself from chuckling. Emma-Lee was her boss's personal assistant, a dynamo of energy that could make even the grumpiest of individuals smile.

"Take heart," Marley said. "He's going to be around for a long time." Well, as long as most drivers stuck around—which wasn't long…normally. "You can bring your die-cast to work tomorrow."

"You're right," Emma-Lee said with an answering grin, blue eyes as bright as a Christmas morning. "I've got all the time in the world. This is going to be *so great*. I can't believe Linc Shepherd is actually going to drive for us."

At least one of them was happy, Marley thought, her smile fading a bit. She'd wanted to kill her brother for hiring the famous driver. But that was the problem with working for a family member—in this instance, the owner of Double S Racing—sometimes you reverted right back to childhood and the days when you were good at ignoring each other—even when you knew the other person was right.

Linc Shepherd should retire.

Everyone in racing knew it. *Sports Scene* magazine had even written a piece about it. After the plane crash that had nearly taken his life two years ago, he'd been out of it. But Linc seemed to think he was as good as new. Unfortunately, one only had to watch Linc walk to know that wasn't true. He'd been in a wheelchair for six months—and it showed. But Gil was convinced Linc still had what it took. Her brother saw "confidence in the man's eyes," whatever that meant.

"You coming down?" Emma-Lee asked, glancing back down the hall as if Linc might be right behind her.

"In a minute or two," Marley said. "I've got something I need to finish."

Emma-Lee nodded, the blond curls she could never seem to tame jiggling around her like birthday ribbons. "I better get going before your brother notices I'm gone," she said. "I just thought you should know Elvis is in the building."

She ducked back out the door before Marley could form a retort.

Elvis, indeed.

Sure there'd been a time back when her brother had first gotten into racing when she'd thought Linc Shepherd was a god. She'd been a naive teenager back then, so consumed by racing that she'd pestered her brother into letting her accompany him into the garage. He'd finally given in, but only because she wouldn't let the matter drop: she'd had a massive crush on Linc and nothing was going to keep her from meeting him. Not anymore. Lord, she still couldn't believe how idiotic she'd been. After everything she'd done to gain his attention, she wouldn't blame Linc if he took one look at her and ran in the other direction—like a trophy elk eluding hunters.

But that was in the past. Time to focus on work.

That proved impossible. If she were honest with herself, she could admit that she was as worked up about Linc's arrival as everyone else at Double S Racing, albeit for different reasons.

"Guess I should just get this over with," she muttered to herself.

"Get *what* over with?"

Marley just about shot out of her chair.

What the hell was he doing in her office?

He was the equivalent of a male panther, right down to the sleek black hair and aloof gray eyes. Those eyes always seemed to smolder whenever gazing at women. In her youth she'd mistaken that gleam as male interest. Now she knew better. Now she recognized what she saw was nothing more than the feral glimmer of a stray cat. Rumor had it he'd had more girlfriends than a male Siamese. When she went to the track these days, she mainly stayed in the sponsor suite, but the few times she'd bumped into him in the garage, he'd always had a gorgeous woman on his arm.

"Linc," she said in what she hoped was a normal voice. "What a surprise," she said.

He had not, she admitted, lost one iota of his sex appeal.

Not one.

"Gil said I should come up and see you. Said you had a big fish on the line."

Big fish? What big fish? What was he talking about?

"That'd be great if you could solidify a sponsorship deal before my first NASCAR Sprint Cup Series race next week."

Sponsorship. Duh. God, what was it with her? Two seconds in his company and she was already losing brain cells. Did his male testosterone suck it right out of her? Was she the equivalent of a stepped-on sponge?

"Um, yeah…" She looked at her computer screen for a moment and tried to recover some of her intellect. "I'm going to try."

It had been years since she'd seen him, she realized. He'd been at the top of his game back then. On the verge of winning a second championship. And then—tragedy. The plane he'd been flying in had crash landed. All on board had been killed, including his best friend.

And yet he claimed to be ready to get back to work again. In vain she searched his eyes for evidence of the killer instinct Gil had talked about. All she saw was a man who seemed just the tiniest bit nervous, maybe even a little scared. That took her aback for a moment.

"Who is it? If you don't mind me asking."

"Actually," she said, "I'd rather not say. At least not until I talk to them some more."

He came into her office then, and the minute he stepped through her door, it was as if a comic book character had entered the room. One of the big ones—like The Incredible Hulk or Wolverine. He made her feel all small and diminutive, the same, damn way she'd felt when she'd been a teenager and she'd crossed paths with him. Over the years she'd attributed that feeling to pubescent hormones.

Guess not.

"Why?" he asked, pulling a chair out and sitting down.

"Shouldn't you be cutting the ribbon on your new car or something?" she asked, trying to maintain her composure. Her gaze found the door, a part of her contemplating the distance between her desk and the exit and how long it'd take for her to get there.

Calm down.

You're acting like a moron. He's just a man. A washed-up race car driver who'd limped as he'd walked toward her. A man who apparently recognized how important she was to him, judging by the anxiety in his eyes.

"I thought it was more important to speak to you. If you've got a potential sponsor interested in financing the No. 459 car, I'll do anything you want. Anything. You just say the word."

I'll do anything.

Had he used the words on purpose? Did he remember

when she'd said pretty much the same thing to *him?* Albeit she'd been trying to get him to notice her and had come up with the brilliant idea of being his personal assistant in order to do so. She would never forget the look on his face when she volunteered for the job.

"Anything?" she repeated softly.

Something in his eyes flickered. He *did* remember.

"Yeah, anything."

It was déjà vu. Only this time she had the upper hand. Back then he'd brushed her off as if she were no more than a summer mosquito that happened to land on his arm. She'd been crushed. Not many days later, Gil had insisted she stay home on race days. She wondered now, as she did back then, if Linc had lodged a complaint about Double S Racing's gawky teenage mascot.

She stood up suddenly, held out her hand. "Good to know, Mr. Shepherd. I'll be certain to take you up on that offer should the need arise. Thank you for stopping by."

Atta girl. Show him who's boss…and that you're no longer a seventeen-year-old girl consumed by puppy love.

"You never answered my question," he said, ignoring her hand and continuing to sit.

She should have recalled then just exactly who this was. A man who made his living by keeping his cool. Someone who was dark and dangerous and predatory toward women. Someone who was good at maintaining the upper hand, despite the fear she saw in his eyes.

How had her brother missed that?

"What question?" she asked, her hand dropping to her side.

He slowly stood, those feral gray eyes of his narrowing a bit. "Who's interested in sponsoring me?"

"And like I said, Mr. Shepherd, I'd really rather not say. At least until the deal progresses a little further."

They were at a standoff, Marley wondering when the last time was someone had stood up to him—specifically a woman. He was such a good-looking man, she would bet he was notoriously spoiled where women were concerned. But she refused to be a doormat. Not again.

"I see," he said.

"Although it's nothing personal," she said, part of her wondering why she was being so secretive. It wasn't like her to withhold information like this, especially from a driver. "I just don't want word to leak out. You know how it is. Someone might hear we're talking to so-and-so and the next thing you know, so-and-so's phone is ringing off the hook with a million *other* people trying to convince so-and-so why *their* driver is the one they should sponsor. It can get crazy."

"Did you tell him about Shelter Home Improvement?"

Marley nearly groaned out loud. What rotten timing.

"You know," her brother added. "I think it'd be great if he went down there with you." At six foot three, Gil Sizemore was a big man and so he filled the doorway much as Linc did, her brother stopping alongside Linc's chair.

"Shelter Home Improvement, huh?" Linc said, his eyes twinkling.

"Down where?" Marley asked, ignoring him.

"Down to Atlanta," he said, "to meet with Shelter Home Improvement."

Linc's gaze settled on her. Was she imagining things, or was that a smile hovering on his lips? She hated when he looked at her like that—as if he was recalling the world's greatest stand-up comedy act, but he wasn't going to share that information with *her*. It was an expression she remembered from her younger years, although back then he'd looked at her like that after she'd offered to wash his race car. She noticed, too, that some of his anxiety had faded. No doubt he was pleased that such a big fish was willing to talk to him about sponsorship.

"Go down to Atlanta with you," Linc said. "That sounds like a *great* idea."

"Actually, I think it might be better if I do that meeting alone."

"Nonsense," Gil said. "Just think what a thrill that'll be for the bigwigs at Shelter Home Improvement. I'll get Emma-Lee started on the arrangements right away."

And then her brother was gone, leaving behind a quiet akin to the stunned silence that followed a pistol blast.

"Ah, yeah. So," she said, taking a deep breath and then immediately wishing she hadn't. She could smell his aftershave—a sort of lemony-pine scent that Marley couldn't help but think smelled nice.

Nice?

She swallowed, trying hard to appear unmoved by his bright, gray eyes. They were a combination of flint and candy. Hard and soft. How was it that after all these years he could still make her gooey inside?

"I guess we'll be attending a meeting together," she

finished when she realized he was waiting for her to say something.

"Yeah. I guess we are."

"I was slated to go down tomorrow. Will that work with your schedule?"

Please, God, don't let it work.

"I'll have to move some things around, but it'll work."

"Great. I'll see you there," she said with a false smile.

"Actually, why don't you let me drive you there?"

She tried to control the escalating beat of her heart. An impossible feat, especially given she had no clue as to why she was suddenly on edge. She wasn't the type of person to let a man's looks affect her, no matter how handsome he was. At least not anymore.

"I don't know if that's a good idea," she said, trying hard to keep her voice even. "It might be better to take separate cars."

"Why? Seems like an awful waste of fuel if we drive down separately." He sat there, looking as smug as a man who knew the woman sitting opposite him still had the hots for him. Which she did. Still.

"I know, but I might take the CEO out to dinner," she said, snatching an excuse out of the air. She aimlessly toyed with a pencil on her desk, the sound of its flat sides a rhythmic click that he seemed to notice, given the way he glanced down at it.

"Then I'll go to dinner with you."

"You don't have to do that."

"I want to," he said, standing suddenly. "No ifs ands or buts about it. I'll pick you up tomorrow. Just have Gil's assistant send over an itinerary."

"No," she said.

"No?" he asked, brows lifted.

"I mean, you can go, but I'm going to drive."

"Marley—"

"Meet me here tomorrow," she said, not giving him time to finish. "In the morning. Early."

He frowned. Marley wondered if he was one of those control freaks who insisted on doing everything for themselves.

"Tomorrow, then," he said, turned to leave the office, Marley feeling as if the strings that held up her shoulder had been suddenly cut, like a marionette in the hands of a nefarious puppet master. What the hell was it about the man—

"By the way," he said, his head popping back into the doorway. "We can share a hotel room, too, if you want."

It felt as if Marley had been deposited on the surface of the sun, that's how hot her face suddenly flamed.

"Well, I—" She took a deep breath. "I mean—"

He burst out laughing.

Marley wanted to sink beneath her desk.

"I'm just kidding, Martian Girl."

She blanched at the use of the nickname he'd given her as a kid.

"See you tomorrow."

Only when he didn't return did Marley put her head in her hands and groan.

Martian Girl.

That's exactly how she felt. Like an alien being inhabited her body because there was no other way to explain how it was that after all these years Marley was attracted to Linc Shepherd.

Still.

"Arrrgggh," she groaned, clutching her head.

CHAPTER TWO

THE DAY DAWNED bright and sunny. Of course it did, Marley thought, the realization irritating the heck out of her. It shouldn't be clear and beautiful outside when inside she was a thunderstorm of chaos.

"You look like a kitten caught in the rain."

Marley looked up from the document she'd been studying—well, not really. Her ability to focus seemed to be nonexistent this morning.

"You ready to go?" she asked, hardly sparing him a glance as she opened her desk drawer, pulled out her purse and stood. "We should head out as soon as possible."

"I'm ready when you are," he said.

She'd been hoping he'd be late. Then she'd be able to leave without him. But a glance at the clock revealed that, like her, he'd been early. It was only 7:50.

"Terrific," she said, sliding past him without looking him in the eye. He had a duffel bag over one shoulder— a vivid reminder that they'd be spending the night in Atlanta—and it reminded her that she had one, too. She paused for a moment. Her briefcase sat in one of the side chairs opposite her desk, a tiny suitcase sitting on the floor.

"Let's go," she said, clutching the briefcase handle in one hand, and the plastic bar of her carry-on luggage in the other. She didn't even wait to see if he would follow, and it was the strangest thing, because as he came up behind her, she felt an inexplicable urge to turn around and see if he was staring at her butt. Stupid. He'd never showed any interest in her before, and so she had no idea why the thought popped into her head that he might *now*. She wore her standard-issue black skirt—knee-length— and a straight cut jacket that matched. Not exactly her most flattering attire, but when they reached the top of the steps that led down to the ground floor of Double S Racing, she couldn't seem to stop herself from glancing back.

He jerked his eyes upward.

She felt her spine snap to attention. "You might want to watch where you're going while we navigate the stairs," she snapped, the unspoken "Not at my rear end" left hanging in the air.

But all the man did was hike up an eyebrow. "Good point," he said softly.

She turned away.

Then right next to her ear, she heard him softly utter, "But I was enjoying the view."

She stumbled.

He kept her from falling down the steps. "Easy there," he said. "Wouldn't want you breaking your pretty little neck."

She jerked out of his arms, wondering how the heck she'd managed to do it again. How had she made a fool of herself?

Just like in the old days.

"Thank you," she said, turning away before he could see her face turn as red as a brake light.

It would be a long trip to Atlanta. Too bad she couldn't make him ride in the trunk.

LINC KNEW he should go easy on her. He really did. But as he followed her out of Double S Racing, he had to fight an urge to step in front of her again, to force her to look into his eyes, to try and understand just where the hell the gawky teenage girl he remembered had gone.

He'd spent all night thinking about her.

Actually, he'd been thinking about how to convince her to let *him* drive. But when he hadn't been thinking about that, he'd found himself recalling their conversation in her office. Frankly, when Gil had told him that Marley was in charge of sponsor relations, it'd almost killed the deal. The last thing he needed was for someone with stalker-like tendencies to be following him around. But Gil had reassured him she wasn't like that anymore, and he'd been right. Honestly, he hadn't recognized the woman who'd greeted him yesterday. Poised, cool, confident, and with slicked-back brown hair that emphasized a stunningly flawless face. She'd pulled it into some kind of fancy bun—very corporate-looking— but he suspected it had the opposite effect of what she intended.

It made her look more beautiful.

"My car's the one with chrome rims," she said, holding her arm out so that the jacket she wore tugged across her chest. The vehicle chirped, drawing his eyes. It was bright outside, the sun's rays refracting off anything with a shiny edge. He had to squint to see the car in question.

She drove an orange Challenger.

"Whoa," he said. "That looks like it could really

burn through fuel. You sure you don't want to take my car?"

"Positive," she said with a smirk, her luggage coasting along behind her. "Looks a lot like the Sixties version, doesn't it?" she asked.

From a distance, it truly did, especially with its black racing stripe. He got hives just thinking about being a passenger in the thing. "I bet your brother had a heart attack when he saw it," he said, more to cover his nervousness than anything else.

She paused. They were in the middle of the parking area, the blacktop beneath their feet already radiating heat. "Why on earth would you say that?"

He glanced at the car again. With its beefy-looking rims and its arrow-like profile, it looked like it belonged on the race track. "Just that you've always seemed to be his darling little sis. I can't imagine he likes you driving a car like that."

"Are you implying it's too much for me to handle?" she asked, walking forward again. She wore heels. They tapped the ground militantly, the sound nearly camouflaged by the sound of her luggage's wheels.

"No," he said. "I'm not inferring that at all." Or was he? "But why don't you let me drive."

"Excuse me?" she said, her briefcase slamming into the side of her leg she stopped so quickly.

The sun highlighted red strands of her hair as she turned back to face him. "Tell me you're not one of those sexist pigs that thinks women can't drive."

"I'm not," he said, lifting his hands. "No way. It's just a long drive. I thought you might like a break."

She released something that sounded like a snort and turned away.

He stood there for a second, staring after her. He had no idea why he felt like a bumbling idiot around her when thirteen years ago all he'd wanted to do was escape her attention. He darted another glance at her.

Not now.

"I wasn't trying to infer you were a poor driver," he said, catching up to her by the back of her car. She opened the trunk, hefted her luggage inside. "I just hate being a passenger."

He'd never admitted that to anyone before, wondered why he did so now, especially to someone who was practically a stranger.

"Throw your duffel in here," was all she told him, motioning toward the black interior and then jerking open the door of her car.

Linc felt his stomach tighten as he did as instructed, telling himself the whole time that he'd be fine. But he almost slammed her trunk closed with more force than necessary, and he jerked open the car door a little too quickly. The smell of new car greeted him, the leather seats offering little traction against his slacks as he slid inside.

"Here we go," she said once he'd buckled up.

He'd rested his hands on his lap, but he felt far from relaxed. It was just a few hours, he told himself. No big deal.

"Listen," she said. "I have some documents in my briefcase there." She pointed over her shoulder with her thumb. "You should probably study them on the way down. Shelter Home Improvement is a big fish and it'd be nice if you made a good impression."

She'd finished backing out, Linc unable to tear his gaze away from the front of the car as she put the vehicle in gear. "I really wish you'd let me drive," he heard himself say.

She slammed on the brake.

He thrust his arms out. "Hey," he cried.

"What is it with you?" she asked. "Are you really so insecure that you feel the need to lord it over women?"

"What?" he asked.

"Why else would you be so insistent on driving? Obviously, you can't stand the fact that I'm in control and you're not." She shook her head. "Typical man."

Linc almost told her the truth. Almost told her what was *really* bothering him, but he couldn't do that. She had his future in his hands, and the last thing he needed was for her to think there was something *wrong* with him.

There wasn't.

He just had a few lingering issues as a result of his plane crash. It was no big deal.

"Actually, I just thought *you* might have some documents to review on the way down," he improvised. "That's all. But by all means, drive if you want to."

She eyed him for a moment before allowing the car to edge forward. "I don't know why I don't believe you, but I don't."

He blanched. Was she able read him so easily? Come to think of it, she *had* known him for an awful long time. Probably longer than any other woman of his acquaintance. Years ago, she'd made a habit of studying him. That might present a problem now.

"Just drive," he said.

She made twin slits out of her eyes before turning her

attention forward. "Documents," she said. "Briefcase. Study them."

"Yes, ma'am," he said. But he couldn't get comfortable in his seat. Even after he'd pulled the papers in question out of her briefcase—a FAQ sheet on Shelter Home Improvement Stores, among other things—he couldn't really focus.

"Does it bother you a lot?"

It took him a moment to process her words. To be honest, he'd been staring at the same FAQ sheet for the better part of fifteen minutes. They'd made it to the freeway already. "What?" he asked.

"The leg," she said, glancing downward before shifting her gaze back to the road.

"Sometimes," he said.

She nodded. "You've been rubbing it ever since you got in the car."

"I have?"

"You have," she reiterated.

Nervous habit, he reasoned. He hadn't even realized he'd been doing it.

"In fact, you look a little white around the mouth."

"It's nothing," he said brusquely. "So," he drawled, trying to change the subject. "Tell me about the meeting we're about to have."

"What do you want to know?" she asked, speeding up as she changed lanes.

It took every ounce of Linc's self-control to appear unfazed by her sudden burst of speed.

"Who are we meeting with? How long will we be there? That kind of thing."

"I expect we'll be there most of the day. We have back-to-back meetings planned with various department heads. Plus, they emailed me this morning to ask if you'd mind stopping by one of their stores. I told them no problem."

"And you think they're serious about sponsoring me?" he asked, trying to focus on the landscape that passed by.

"As serious as anyone I've talked to so far."

"Which means this deal could turn on a dime at a moment's notice."

They crossed beneath an overpass, its reflection beamed back to him via the hood of the car. It was bright outside, but he'd forgotten his sunglasses.

"Which means you'll have to work hard to sell yourself."

He nodded, his right hand finding the edge of the car seat. He clung to it despite his best efforts.

"Linc, what's wrong?"

His gaze shot to her. "Wrong? What could possibly be wrong?"

"You're as jumpy as a toy poodle."

"I am not."

She kept sneaking glances at him, and he could tell by the look on her face that she didn't believe him. And then she shifted lanes. She did so quickly and suddenly it caused Linc to cry out in surprise.

"You are on edge," she accused, guiding the car off the freeway.

"What are you doing?"

"Pulling over."

"Why?" he asked.

"Because there's something wrong and I want to know what. My brother's worked *way* too hard to get

Double S Racing off the ground to have a washed-up driver bring it down."

"I'm not washed up."

She pulled over at the bottom of an off ramp, a group of commercial buildings across the intersection to his right. Other cars drove by, their drivers staring at them curiously. Marley flicked on her hazard lights.

"Are you on drugs?"

"Drugs?" he cried, abashed to realize that he felt better now that she'd stopped. "Don't be ridiculous."

She leaned toward him. "Don't lie to me, Linc. Something has you wound up tighter than a rubber band and I want to know what."

He glanced outside the car. The sound of vehicles zooming by was a rhythmic swish-swish-swish of noise. "I don't like being in the passenger seat."

"That does it," she said. "If you can't be honest with me maybe we should turn around and head back to the shop. I can tell Shelter Home Improvement there's been a snafu."

"No," he said quickly, sharply. "Don't do that."

Her eyes were hard as she asked, "Then what is it?"

He looked away for a second, wondered how much to tell her, then decided he owed her the truth. "Ever since the accident, I've had issues."

He saw her draw back, the seat belt she wore going slack for a moment. "What kind of issues?"

"I wasn't kidding when I said I don't like being in the passenger seat. I get…anxious."

"How anxious?"

He debated for a moment, felt the urge to pull on the

door handle and flee the car. He controlled that urge by sheer force of will. "I've been diagnosed with anxiety disorder."

CHAPTER THREE

"ANXIETY DISORDER?" Marley repeated, and she had to force herself to keep from yelling. "And you're telling us about this *now?*"

"It's no big deal. It has nothing to do with my driving."

She collapsed against her seat. "Good heavens," she murmured. "Please tell me you've got this under control."

When she finally opened her eyes, it was in time to see him staring at her, the look on his face one that could only be called acute misery.

Linc Shepherd, humiliated.

She never would have thought it possible. But if she were honest with herself, it went a long way toward leveling the playing field.

He wasn't a god.

Not that she'd ever actually thought of him that way, but she'd lived through humiliation after humiliation thanks to him, and so it was nice to see the tables turned.

"Are you in therapy?"

She saw his jaw thrust forward. "I was."

She shook her head. "We should probably work that into one of our press releases," she said. "I'll talk to PR about it. I'm sure they can spin it. Make it into a human interest story. Driver battles anxiety in order to return to racing."

"I don't want this publicized."

"Linc," she said. "We can't hide your disorder."

"It's not a disorder. It's completely manageable as long as *I* drive."

She laughed—she couldn't stop herself—but she immediately regretted it. He appeared so obviously miserable about his little problem that sympathy won out. "Okay. Fine. You drive."

"Thank you," he said quickly and emphatically.

"But if you wreck it, you buy it," she said, releasing her seat belt.

"Please," he scoffed, looking less and less uncomfortable.

"And I still say we need to leak this out somehow. Don't worry," she said quickly. "We'll do it in such a way that you won't be emasculated."

"I'm not worried about that," he said.

"Then what is it?"

He looked ahead, Marley recognizing that he'd grown more handsome over the years. Amazing that he'd stayed single all this time. She knew for a fact that he'd had more than his fair share of women throw themselves at him.

"I just don't want people to make a big deal about this. The accident—" She saw his jaw thrust forward again, saw his hands clench in his lap. "It was a bad time in my life. This little problem I have," he shook his head, "it's just part of it all. I'm trying to move forward and so the last thing I want is a bunch of media types, or Anxiety Disorder International asking me to be their spokesperson."

She found herself smiling before she could stop herself. "Is there really an Anxiety Disorder International?"

He met her gaze, and for the first time since they'd been reintroduced, she saw humor in that gaze. Genuine humor, not the sarcastic kind. Actually, now that she thought about it, it was the first time he'd *ever* looked at her like that.

"I have no idea," he said.

It was her turn to stare out the front windshield. The sun had moved higher into the sky and the glare was killing her eyes. "Okay, fine," she said. "We'll keep it under wraps, but I need you to prove to me that you're really fine."

"Just give me the keys," he said, holding out his hand.

Five minutes later they were on their way, and five minutes after that, Marley had her answer. He was completely at ease behind the wheel of her car. She relaxed a little inside. For a few moments there she'd been thinking they might have a huge problem. Thank goodness that turned out not to be true.

But *anxiety disorder?*

She'd never heard of a man having that. Sure, she supposed it happened, but not to a race car driver.

"When did you first notice this little problem?"

"Once I learned how to walk again…and drive."

She winced inwardly. Though she'd heard about the accident—who on planet Earth hadn't?—she'd never really given it any serious thought other than how sad it was for all families involved. But afterward, when the headlines had faded, she was abashed to realize she hadn't given him another thought. Well, that wasn't true. Every once in a while his name would come up in conversation, but beyond that, she'd hardly noticed what was going on in his life.

He'd had to learn to walk again.

She might not like the man very much, but she couldn't imagine what that must have been like. And she couldn't imagine the stress he must be under right now. Anyone in the racing industry would tell you there was a lot of pressure on a driver to succeed. Not only was he battling that, but he also had to deal with a bum leg and an apparent psychological disorder—although apparently he'd been telling her the truth. She could see no sign of stress on his face now.

"See," he said, glancing at her. "I told you I'd be fine."

"I know," she said, wondering why she felt so strange all of a sudden. "But you understand why I had to be certain you were telling me the truth?"

"I do," he said.

"And you're going to promise me right now that you're not about to climb into a race car while on some kind of anxiety drug."

"I told you," he said after shooting her another glance. "It's not like that. As long as I'm in the driver's seat, I'm fine."

"Are you worried?" she found herself asking.

"About what?" he asked, his blue eyes intense.

"That you're not going to make it."

It was the wrong question to ask him. If he hadn't been on the freeway, he probably would have slammed on the brakes. "There's not a single doubt," he said, his voice terse. "Not a single one, that I'm as good a driver—maybe even better—than I was before."

And yet, still, she felt the need to push him. "Better how?" she asked, genuinely curious.

He didn't answer right away. His face was in profile, but she could see his mind tossing over her question. "I appreciate things more."

It wasn't the answer she'd expected. Linc had always been one of those drivers many had called cocky. Honestly, it was part of the reason why she'd been so horrified by her behavior in the past. Once the puppy love had worn off, she'd found herself wondering what she ever saw in the man. Sure, he was good-looking. Okay, *really* good-looking, but she didn't like men who were full of themselves, and that was the impression she'd always gotten over the years.

"I can understand how something like that accident could change your life."

She saw his shoulders relax. "It does."

And though she knew she might regret the words, she found herself saying. "I'll do whatever I can to help you get back on top."

His eyes found her own again. "Will you?"

She nodded, having to look away for some reason. They were passing a residential area, trees intermixed with homes and lawns. Nice homes, she absently noted.

"Given how I treated you when you were younger, I appreciate that."

She quickly turned her head toward him. "I was young. Silly," she quickly amended. "A kid with a stupid teenage crush. Thank god I grew out of it."

"Did you?"

She wished the radio was on. A song. A broadcaster. One of those annoying ads. Anything that might help her change the topic of their conversation. "Of course I did," she said. And then she leaned forward, pressing the power button before she could stop herself. "Hope you like country music."

"I do," he said, but there it was again, that look in his eyes, the one of secret amusement.

"Good," she said, hoping, wishing, praying that he might drop the subject because the truth of the matter was, she hated being in the car with him. Hated the fact that it was just the two of them.

She wasn't over her crush.

The sexual attraction was still there. Raw. Unfettered. Uncontrollable.

Because from the moment he'd climbed into the car she'd been aware—of him, of the tangy scent of his aftershave, of the way his tall frame filled the car.

Damn it.

She didn't need this. Didn't want to be attracted to him…still. What she wanted was to get this stupid business trip over with because the sooner she secured a major sponsor, the sooner he'd be out of her hair.

She just hoped that happened before she did something to embarrass herself.

THEY ARRIVED in Atlanta beneath sunny skies. Actually, Linc thought, the whole trip had been pleasant. Once he'd quit grilling her about her crush on him, she'd seemed to settle down.

But he'd seen the look in her eyes.

No matter what she might say, there was still residual attraction. She tried like the devil to hide it, but it was still there.

He smiled to himself as he followed her directions

to Shelter Home Improvement's headquarters. They were just outside of Atlanta, high rises gleaming in the distance like giant crystals. One thing Linc had come to realize over the years was that the entire southern United States looked about the same. And so, just like North Carolina, they were surrounded by smooth green pastures intermixed with thick stands of trees. And just like up north, contractors chose to erect their buildings in whatever treeless pasture they could find. The headquarters of Shelter Home Improvement had been built in one of those clearings, its massive concrete-and-glass enclave seeming to sprout up from nowhere.

He was nervous.

Linc found himself wiping his palms against the front of his tan slacks as he slipped out of Marley's car.

"Catch," he said, tossing her the keys across the hood of her car.

"Hey," she complained, having to dive to catch them. "If that had landed on my car, you'd have been paying for a new paint job."

"That's why I was aiming for your head."

She tucked the keys into her purse, Linc thinking that even her car's engine smelled new. He caught a whiff of barely broken-in motor as he stood waiting for her.

"Thanks a lot," she said, giving him a smile that was completely devoid of animosity. At least they'd progressed that far. He glanced at the building ahead of him. They'd parked in the visitors' stalls and so they were right in front of the two-story structure, its windows tinted with something that turned them blue-black. The building's roofline was framed by green and black paint—the same color as Shelter Home Improvement's logo. If things went right, those would be the colors of his car.

If things went right.

"You look nervous," she said, her briefcase hanging against her upper thigh. She wore a black business suit that should have made her look severe; instead, it hugged her curves in a way that attracted his eyes. When had she grown into such a beautiful woman?

"Not nervous," he said, "just anxious."

"Isn't that the same thing?"

He shook his head, stepping up next to her as she headed toward the front door. "I equate anxiousness with anticipating an event, and I'm really looking forward to meeting the people from Shelter Home Improvement— in a good way."

She paused before a set of double doors with the company's logo drawn onto the glass. The stare she gave him was one of calm reassurance. "You know, if this doesn't work out I have other fish on the line."

"Yeah, but none as big as Shelter Home Improvement."

She nibbled her lower lip. Funny, he'd forgotten she did that until now. Years ago he'd considered the gesture childish, now he couldn't keep his eyes off her soft flesh.

"True," she said, "but it's not like it would be the end of the world if they said no."

He looked away, out into the parking area. "I realize that," he said. "And after almost losing my life, you'd think I'd be more immune to this kind of pressure."

She clasped his arm. "It'll be okay. You'll see."

He hoped she was right, Linc thought, following her into the building.

They were immediately enveloped by a cool, conditioned air, Linc's bare arms instantly sprouting goose bumps. He wore a Double S Racing polo shirt and matching tan slacks but he was wondering if he shouldn't have put on a sports jacket instead.

"Welcome to Shelter Home Improvement," the receptionist, a woman with black hair and bright green eyes said. She sat behind a massive counter painted the same green as the building outside. In fact, the entire lobby echoed the color. Marble tile. Lush plants. A plush couch covered in a fabric that reminded Linc of money. Even the pictures that hung on the wall—exterior shots of various Shelter Home Improvement stores—echoed the hue.

"Who are you here to see today?" the woman asked, her gaze shifting to him. She jerked out of her chair. "Oh my gosh. You're Linc Shepherd," she cried, the cord that ran from the communication console to her ear pulled taut so that she almost tipped over.

"I am," Linc said, catching Marley's amused expression.

"You're here," the woman wearing a name tag engraved Nancy said.

"He's here," Marley echoed. "And *we're* here to see Sharon Taylor." But the words were uttered in a teasing way.

The receptionist sank back down. "Oh. A…yeah. Sure. Of course you are."

Linc bit back a smile. He was used to being recognized, but it'd been a while since someone had reacted so strongly. He took it as a good sign that it'd happened at Shelter Home Improvement's headquarters.

The receptionist dialed some numbers, the keypad

emitting beeps. "Would you please tell Ms. Taylor that Mr. Shepherd and Ms...." She glanced at Marley in panic.

"Ms. Sizemore," Marley provided.

"Sizemore," the woman said, "are here to see her." The receptionist's eyes grew unfocused as she listened to the person on the other end. "Okay, great," the woman said with a wide smile. "I'll tell them." She hung up. "Ms. Taylor will be right down."

"Great," Marley said.

"We're meeting with a woman?" Linc said as they turned away, Marley leading him to the sofa he'd noticed earlier. It was every bit as comfortable as he'd anticipated.

"Do you have a problem with that, Mr. Shepherd?"

"No, of course not," he said, but she was teasing him. He relaxed. "I just thought we were meeting with the CEO."

"Sharon *is* the CEO."

Linc felt his brows lift. "Really."

She laughed then. "Why, Linc Shepherd," she said, her Charleston accent so pronounced that she sounded exactly like the Southern belle that, in fact, she was. "I had no idea you were such a sexist pig."

"I'm not sexist," he said. "Just surprised. And stop calling me sexist, would you? That's twice today. I'm not a blue-blooded gentleman who thinks women should stay home and raise babies."

She looked suitably chastened. "No, I suppose you're not," she said, but whatever else she was about to say was cut off by a woman's voice.

"Ms. Sizemore," someone said. "How nice to finally meet you face-to-face."

Linc found himself turning, his attention snagged by the stunningly beautiful woman who walked toward them, hand outstretched.

"Ms. Taylor," Marley said. "It's good to finally put a face with the name, too."

The moment the woman released her hand, she was turning to him and Linc recognized the look in the woman's eyes as one he'd seen countless times before.

Blatant invitation.

This woman had more than sponsoring him in mind, which is why he uttered a silent *uh-oh*.

CHAPTER FOUR

"Ms. TAYLOR, this is Linc Shepherd," Marley said, something coiling deep in her stomach at the look in the woman's eyes. If Linc had been an ice cream cone, it was obvious Sharon Taylor would have gobbled him up.

She released a breath of impatience. This might be a long day.

"Call me Sharon," she said with a smile. She had a mole next to her mouth. Marley thought it looked like a tick.

"How do you do, Sharon?" Linc said, his smile seeming to be abashed—as if he were embarrassed by the woman's obvious interest.

"Thank you for meeting with us today," Marley said, wondering what to do. Should she inject herself between Linc and Sharon? Try to tell the woman with her eyes to back off? Leave it alone? "Linc's really excited about meeting some of your staff," she added.

She spared Marley a glance for about 1.5 milliseconds, the blond ponytail she wore flicking back and forth as she moved her head.

"And we're excited to have him," Sharon said, drawing up to her full height. She must have been six feet tall—she stood almost eye to eye with Linc—her sleek body shown to advantage in a black business suit. Unlike Marley who was barely average height. "And might I just say, I'm a really huge fan, Mr. Shepherd. I was so saddened by your accident. How's the leg feeling, by the way?"

She touched his upper arm—as if in sympathy—but Marley saw the way her thumb lightly stroked Linc's bare flesh.

"It's fine," he said, his eyes snagging Marley's attention. Clearly, he'd spotted the interest in Ms. Taylor's eyes, too. "Thanks for asking."

"I'm so glad to hear that. We wouldn't want any lingering issues getting in the way of your driving now, would we?"

It wasn't the words that set Marley's teeth on edge— after all, as a potential sponsor, she had a right to ask such a question—it was more the look on her face. She seemed about ready to volunteer her services should Linc need physical therapy.

Yeesh.

"Who are we meeting with today?" Marley asked, trying to refocus the conversation on the matter at hand.

"Just me," Sharon said brightly.

Therein ensued what was, for Marley, a painful hour while she was forced to endure Sharon's false enthusiasm (or *was* it false?). When it was time to break for lunch, Marley couldn't get out of there fast enough.

"You sure you don't want to grab a bite to eat with us?" Marley felt compelled to ask.

"I wish I could," Sharon said with a disappointed smile. "But we'll connect again in about an hour when I take Linc on a tour of one of our stores. Afterwards we'll head out for dinner."

Marley had known that was the plan. Still, she was

forced to sound excited as she said, "No problem. We'll see you in an hour, then."

But the moment they stepped into the warm sunshine she couldn't stop herself from saying, "Jeesh. I think I just witnessed the world record. I've never seen a woman bat her eyelashes more times in the space of an hour." Marley stabbed the unlock button on her key chain more forcefully than necessary.

"Really?" Linc said, sounding surprised. "I didn't notice anything out of the ordinary."

That stopped Marley in her tracks. "You're kidding, right?" she asked, but they were forced to move forward when a car headed toward them. They stopped in front of her car, Marley handing the keys to Linc absently. "Linc," Marley mimicked. "I'm you're biggest fan."

Linc laughed. "She didn't say that."

Marley's teeth ground in irritation. "No," Marley reluctantly admitted. "Not those words exactly, but she couldn't have been more obvious. She has the hots for you."

"Does not," Linc said as he headed for the driver's side door.

Marley didn't move. "You've got to be joking. You're telling me you didn't notice."

"No," Linc said, opening the door and sliding inside.

Marley had no choice but to do the same, but once she'd settled into the slick leather seat and pulled on her seat belt, she muttered, "Then you're blind."

Linc laughed again. "And you're sounding awfully jealous."

She jerked upright so hard the seat belt checked her

in the neck. She grimaced and pulled the thing away from her skin. "Don't be ridiculous."

"Where are we going?" he asked.

She waved a hand imperiously. "I don't care. You decide. Something fast. I wouldn't want you to be late for Little Miss Biggest Fan."

He rested a hand on the steering wheel and turned toward her. "You really don't like her, do you?"

Marley drew back. It finally registered that she sounded like a jealous harpy. Lord help her. Half a day in the man's company had her right back where she'd started years ago…lusting after Linc Shepherd.

You are not *lusting after him.*

But wasn't she? Just a tiny bit? If she were honest with herself she'd have to admit she found him sexy. Frankly, she really didn't blame Sharon for batting her lashes at him.

"I'm just worried she might have an ulterior motive in wanting to sponsor you."

He still didn't start the car. Marley hoped that he would, and that he'd drop the subject. Because the way he was looking at her sent a frisson of awareness through her that had her wishing she could roll down her window.

"You're worried I find Sharon attractive."

"I am not!"

He smirked.

"Linc, stop it," she said, sitting upright and straightening her jacket. "I'm no more worried about that than I am jealous. Now. Let's get going. We only have an hour."

Dratted man *still* didn't start the car.

"You still want me."

Her entire body burst into flames, from the tip of her toes to the top of her needed-some-new-highlights hair. "Let's go," she repeated, deadpan.

"You still want me and you're angry that someone else wants me, too."

"Linc—"

He covered her mouth with his hands. Marley gasped, drew back. He followed her, the scent of his fingers filling her nostrils. Hand soap. That's what he smelled like.

"Face it, you're still smitten with me."

She shook her head.

He smirked.

She darted sideways, all but yelling, "Don't touch me."

That was when he decided to start the car. Marley heard his deep chuckle over the sound of the engine.

"This is turning out to be an interesting day."

"I mean it, Linc, if you ever touch me like that again…" But he backed the car out of its parking spot so fast she found herself yelping in surprise.

"What?" he asked, giving her a movie star grin. "What will you do?"

"Ask Gil to have you fired."

He shook his head. "You won't do that."

"Yes, I will."

"Because if you do," he said, droning on as if she'd never spoken, "you'll have to admit the reason why." He wagged his eyebrows at her devilishly.

"I refuse to discuss the matter with you further."

"Because you know I'm right."

"Just drive," she said, fed up with the situation.

Humiliation. That's what she felt. Because deep down she knew he was right.

"Should we just skip lunch and head right to a hotel?"

That did it.

"Stop it," she said firmly. "I don't know what makes you think I haven't outgrown my crush on you, but I have. So, please, let's do our best to keep things on a professional level, okay? My job is to find you a sponsor, and come hell or high water, I'm going to do that. But if you make this difficult for me, if you insist on giving me grief about my past, I'll hand your sponsorship problem over to another person, someone less qualified. Someone who might not succeed where I will."

The words had the desired effect. She saw his mouth tighten, the smile evaporating like water on hot asphalt.

"That sounded suspiciously like a threat," he said.

"It was."

He pulled onto the main road. "Where to?" he asked again.

"Anywhere," she said.

And wished anywhere could be far away from him. Despite her show of bravado, Marley knew she wouldn't do as she threatened. She was too much of a professional for that. But she'd had to get him to stop. If he'd kept up his teasing, she might have done something foolish, like tell him he was right.

She still wanted him. Badly.

But she could never admit that. Not now. Not ever. She'd already made a fool of herself over him once before. She refused to do so again.

THE VISIT to the local Shelter Home Improvement store proved to be as difficult to endure as their first meeting with Sharon. But the difficulty was no doubt compounded by the tension between her and Linc. They'd managed to get through their lunch, despite the fact that Marley had lost her appetite. But they were *both* on edge as they finished up the tour.

"I'll see you later tonight," Sharon said with a wide smile as they stood outside the store.

"Thank you so much for your time." Linc smiled politely.

"You're welcome," Sharon said, her eyes sliding up and down Linc in a way that made Marley want to shout, "See! See what she just did!"

But Marley couldn't do that. Instead she moved forward and held out her hand. "See you at dinner tonight."

She was beyond relieved when they were finally allowed to walk away.

"Whew, I'm glad that's over," Linc said when they were outside and on their way to Marley's car—no, unofficially Linc's car—as the sun started to sink beneath the horizon. "You were right," Linc said. "Sharon's interest in me *is* more than professional."

Marley drew up short. "You see it now?"

Linc nodded. "I do."

Her shoulders went slack with relief. "I'm so glad to hear you say that."

"I thought for sure she'd hand me her phone number before we left," Linc said.

"She was something else all right."

They were in a shadow, and Linc's afternoon razor stubble more pronounced. Damn, but he was sexy-looking. She blinked, then immediately chastised herself for having such a thought.

Not again, remember? she reminded herself.

"Oh, well," Linc said. "At least we get a free dinner."

Marley nodded. They were eating at The Plantation, a posh restaurant located along the outskirts of Atlanta. A former tobacco farm, the owners had converted the two-story antebellum mansion into one of the city's best restaurants, with spacious suites upstairs, excellent food…at least according to the website.

"Maybe we should make the best of it," Marley said.

"Truce?" Linc asked, holding out a hand.

Marley stared at the limb, remembering the way his fingers felt against her mouth. Her body warmed up all over again. "Truce," she said, taking his hand.

It felt like clasping an electric fence. Marley had never touched him before, not like this. Their eyes connected. Marley saw his lashes flicker, quickly, but then he was looking away and stepping back.

"I suppose we should head on over to The Plantation and check in," he said. He didn't wait for a response, just made a beeline for the car. Marley was left standing there wondering what had just happened.

Had he felt it, too?

It sure seemed that way, at least judging by the look in his eyes. Something had sparked in the depths of his gray eyes, something that'd made adrenaline rush through Marley's veins.

The drive over was quiet, Marley trying her best to think of something to say. In the end she gave up. If he didn't want to talk, she wouldn't push it.

A few minutes later they pulled into a long drive lined by ancient trees. Sharon had suggested they stay there and Marley could understand why. The lavish interior with its twenty-foot ceilings featured a number of extravagant floral arrangements that took her breath away, one smack in the middle of the marble foyer. A black-clad lobby attendant pointed them toward the reservation desk. She was never more glad than when the hotel checked them in quickly.

"I'll meet you here in two hours." She handed Linc his own room key.

"Marley," he said softly.

Her whole body reacted to the timbre of his voice. The way he'd said her name…it sounded almost like a plea. When she looked into his eyes she saw something in his gaze, something that she'd never seen before. Desire?

Her heart began to pound. "Yes?"

But as quickly as the look came, it faded. "Thanks for doing this for me," he said.

That wasn't what he'd been about to say. She would bet her life on it. "You're welcome," she said.

"I mean it." He ran a hand through his hair. "You're really good at your job."

"Thank you," she said.

Had that been interest in his eyes? Was it possible? Could he be attracted to her?

"I'll see you later," he said, turning and walking away before she could reply.

"Yeah," she heard herself mutter as she watched him disappear from view. "Later."

AFTER TWO HOURS PASSED, an anxious Marley left her room with her heart in her throat. Every time she recalled the look in Linc's eyes, her pulse began to pound.

That had been interest in his eyes. She was certain of it.

She found Linc standing by the entrance to the restaurant, his black pants hugging a body still honed by fitness, despite his injuries.

"Hi," she said softly.

"Hello," he said right back, eyeing her up and down.

And, okay, she could admit it. She'd dressed up for him. When she'd packed this morning she'd grabbed a dress that she knew set her figure off to advantage. It was black with a neckline that showed enough to snag a man's interest, but not so much that it could be deemed unprofessional.

"You look nice," he said.

"Thank you," she said, looking around for Sharon, who obviously hadn't arrived yet. "You look nice, too," she added.

He wore an off-white button-down shirt that turned his skin a honey brown. He had smile wrinkles near the corners of his eyes, she noticed, and a tiny scar on his forehead. Was it from the accident?

"Should we go on in?" she asked, because whenever she thought of what he'd been through, her stomach twisted. No matter how much she'd tried to loathe him over the years, she'd never quite managed to pull it off. And so when she'd heard about the wreck, she'd been overcome by emotion. She wouldn't wish something like that on her worst enemy.

"I don't see why not," Linc said. "We can ask the maître d' to show her to our table."

Perhaps they should wait, Marley found herself thinking, but Linc was already off arranging matters. She wouldn't mind sitting down. She hated standing around making small talk. At least if they were seated, she could pretend to be interested in her menu.

"Off we go," Linc said when he returned a few moments later.

What other scars did he live with? she wondered. Besides the limp and his inability to sit in a passenger seat? But then she caught a glimpse of the room they were entering and she almost drew up short.

"Wow," Marley said as they were shown to their table. A number of heads turned as they crossed along the lush carpet, but Marley wasn't certain if that was because of Linc's good looks, or because he was instantly recognizable to NASCAR fans.

"This looks great," Linc said, taking a seat opposite her.

"It does," Marley echoed, instantly using the huge menu to shield her face. But as it turned out, they didn't have long to wait.

"Don't you just love this place?" Sharon announced as she approached.

Marley heard Linc say, "It's beautiful, Sharon. And the food smells scrumptious."

"Well, you better order champagne to go with your meal because I have some terrific news."

And Marley's heart stopped. She set her menu down.

"Linc," Sharon said after she took her seat and pulled closer to Linc. "I just got off the phone with our chairman of the board. It's unanimous. Shelter Home Improvement has agreed to a two-year sponsorship."

Marley felt her breath catch.

But she wasn't prepared for the emotion she saw in Linc's eyes. There was such a profound look of gratitude—and relief—that Marley felt tears come to her eyes.

"Congratulations," Sharon said, having obviously spotted the same thing because she leaned in and squeezed his upper arm. Her nails were painted bright red, Marley suddenly noticed.

"Thank you," Linc said.

When the champagne came, they lifted their glasses, clinking them and making the crystal ring.

"To a long and successful business venture," Marley said.

"I'll drink to that," Linc said.

Perhaps it was relief. Perhaps it was how horribly she struggled with keeping her emotions in check, but for whatever reason, she found herself drinking a bit more than usual. She was pretty fuzzy-headed by the time they finished dinner. That was unusual for her because she never, ever drank during business dinners. It was unprofessional.

"I think I should probably have some water," Marley said when Sharon tried to pour her another glass.

"Don't be silly," she said. "Let's drink this down," but she had eyes only for Linc.

"Actually, I think I'm going to retire for the evening. We have to head back to town early tomorrow morning and so I think I should get some shut-eye," Linc said.

They did not have to leave early, but Marley wasn't about to argue the point. Obviously, Linc really had come to the realization that Sharon was doing her best to attract his interest and was trying to put a stop to things.

"I should head upstairs, too," Marley said.

There was nothing Sharon could say to that, at least not without sounding rude, and so Marley found herself standing, her upper body wobbling a bit. Linc came around and steadied her with his hand.

"Easy there," Linc said. "Your brother will have my hide if I let something happen to you."

Sharon's eyes widened at the familiarity of the gesture, so much so that Marley found herself saying, "Linc's like a big brother to me," as they walked out. "I've known him since I was a teenager."

"Really?" Sharon asked, seeming a bit appeased by the explanation.

"In fact, I used to have the biggest crush on him." She opened her arms wide, nearly clocking Linc in the nose. "Ooo. Sorry," she said.

They were in the main lobby now. Linc had to steady her again when they came to a stop.

"I'll just bet you did," Sharon said, eyeing the two of them together.

"But he rejected me and I got mad." It was one of those moments when you know you've had too much to drink, but you can't help saying the first thing that pops into your mind. "So I set his race car on fire."

"You did what?" Sharon cried.

Marley nodded, swaying a bit. She knew she would hear about this later, but hoped Sharon wouldn't think any less of Double S Racing when the head of sponsor relations was clearly tipsy.

Oh, well.

"Yup," she said. "Threw a shop rag inside and lit it on fire."

"You're kidding," Sharon said, sounding more and more horrified.

"I didn't mean to catch the whole *thing* on fire," she said. "I just wanted to scorch Linc's custom race seat."

"But one of the techs had just used degreaser to clean off the interior," Linc provided.

"Oh, no," Sharon said.

"It, too, caught on fire," Marley admitted.

"Before we knew it, the whole car went up in flames," Linc said.

"*Not* one of my best moments," Marley said.

"I bet not," Sharon said, appearing genuinely amused.

"She was a major pain in my rear when she was younger."

Was it the champagne she had ingested, or was that a look of tenderness in Linc's eyes. No way. She was definitely imagining it.

"Anyway," Linc said. "I always try to keep an eye out for her."

"How sweet," Sharon said, but it was obvious she didn't really think that. She looked at Marley as more of an imposition, Marley could tell.

"He is, isn't he?" Marley said, painting a look of adoration on her face.

"I guess we'll find out," Sharon said, suddenly all business. "Thank you for joining me for dinner," she said to Marley. "Linc, we look forward to working with you."

"Same here," Linc said.

And then they were alone.

"Come on," Linc said. "Let's get you to your room."

But when he turned away, Marley was struck by the notion that she didn't want this night to end and, even more shockingly, that yet again her crush had come back—full force, and that she was just tipsy enough to act on it.

"Oh, dear," she heard herself mutter.

CHAPTER FIVE

LINC KNEW she was tipsy. "What?" he asked. "Are you going to be sick?"

She shook her head, but on her face was a look of horror akin to someone who'd just seen an apparition. "I'm fine," she said softly.

"Uh-huh," he said, hooking his arm through hers so he could lead her past the registration desk.

"Don't," she said quickly.

He glanced down at her in surprise, and now she was frowning up at him. "I can walk just fine."

Aha. She was the type of person that believed there was nothing wrong with them when, in fact, there was. "Just the same," he said, "I'm going to walk you to your room."

"No," she said with a sharp shake of her head. "I do not need your assistance." When she noticed him staring down skeptically, she added, "But I thank you kindly for your offer."

Linc nearly smiled. She sounded just like Scarlett O'Hara. And for a moment he found himself wondering what she'd look like with soft curls atop her head, maybe even a low-cut ball gown—

And where the hell had *that* thought come from?

"Where's your key?" he asked her.

She shook her head—as if arguing with herself over

something—then fished around in her purse and handed the thing over without a word.

"I'm in the Flower Room," Marley said.

"I know," Linc said. He'd heard the receptionist tell her that earlier.

"Come on," he said, lightly touching her arms.

He led her toward a stairwell as wide as a car; plum-colored carpet padded their steps. He had to hold on to the banister at the same time he gripped her arm. She didn't pull away this time, seeming to recognize that she needed some guidance. While she wasn't drunk, she was definitely tipsy. Her hair had started to come loose. As if she'd scratched at it absently when he hadn't been looking. The light brown strands swooped around her face gently, softening it. She had sweeping brows, the kind usually found on models or actresses. They framed her eyes in a way that highlighted their unique color.

Now, now, Linc...keep your thoughts out of the gutter.

Because he couldn't help but admit that after today, he saw her in whole new light. She'd handled herself so professionally throughout the hours, and yet beneath the cool exterior he'd caught a glimpse of the headstrong youth she'd been years ago. When he looked back at that time, he had to admit he'd been amused by the whole situation. And, yes, secretly flattered. She was just a kid, but *boy*, had she ever had the hots for him.

Did she still?

Stop staring at her.

He knew he should heed the voice. She was years younger than him. Too young. Plus, he doubted his new boss would welcome Linc getting involved with his kid sister. Just what he needed. To get off on the wrong foot with Gil before his professional relationship with him even started. But he couldn't deny that earlier, as they'd stood in the lobby below, there'd been a moment when he'd found himself wondering what it'd be like to touch her. Too bad he felt honor-bound to stay away from her.

"Here we go," he said, turning at the top of the stairs.

You will not *touch her.*

He knew he wouldn't. Not that she appeared to have anything other than getting to her room on her mind.

"Which one is yours?" she asked.

"I'm at the end of the hall. You're right next door."

"Oh," she said.

He opened the door for her, but she didn't move once the green light beeped.

"What is it?" he asked.

She met his gaze then and Linc knew he was doomed.

"Don't go," she said softly.

"Marley—"

"I saw the look in your eyes earlier," she interjected. "The one you tried so hard to conceal. You were thinking about what it'd be like to go to bed with me."

How the hell had she figured *that* out?

"You forget I've known you for years," she said, seeming to read his mind…again. "And I've wondered the same thing, too, oh so many times."

He swallowed.

She tipped her chin up. "I want to find out."

"No," he said. "It's a bad idea. Your brother—"

"Won't care," she said. "Especially if we keep this to ourselves."

But what if he *did* find out? What if Gil learned he'd seduced his little sister. He knew he was protective of her. Everyone in the garage knew that. Linc had a feeling Gil wouldn't be happy with the two of them hooking up. Not now. Not with so much on the line. Hell, he had a career to relaunch.

"I can't," he said.

She pressed a hand against his chest. He swallowed again.

But what if *she* seduced *him?* That wouldn't be his fault now, would it?

"Yes, you can," she said, her hand sliding down his belly, but she didn't go any further than his waistline. Instead she clasped his hand, holding on to it as she took her room key away from him, then turned and opened her door.

"Come on," she said softly.

Marley heard the door close behind them.

This couldn't be happening, she found herself thinking.

After so many teenage fantasies, she wasn't really here, now, about to make love to him.

He pulled her up against him, her back crushed against his chest.

She sighed. She was.

He turned her quickly. Their lips connected and Marley's mouth opened before she could stop herself.

Chocolate. He tasted like dessert. A slice of mousse. And then he was pressing his body up against hers, Marley's head tipping sideways as his mouth slid to the left and trailed kisses down her jaw...

She shivered.

And her ear…

She shivered again.

His teeth found her neck. "Linc," she whispered.

He bit her. Not hard, but enough that she moaned, her hands finding his shirt, her fingers running over the taut ridges of his chest that she could feel through the fabric that covered him. She wanted him to take the thing off, wanted to run her mouth over his flesh.

"Marley," he said, his hands moving to her shoulders. She thought he might push her away as he drew back for a moment. "Are you on birth control?" he asked.

Every muscle in his body relaxed, then just as quickly tensed again. "Yes," she said.

"Good," he said, pushing her back toward the bed. Marley knew—she just knew—where this would end.

And she didn't care.

Lord help her, she just didn't care.

CHAPTER SIX

HE'D SLEPT with her.

Linc resisted the urge to roll to the edge of the bed, cover his head and groan.

Morning had dawned.

Bright, nearly neon light blasted in from the windows to his left. They hadn't even bothered to close the blinds last night, that's how all-consuming their lovemaking had been.

What had he done?

His new boss would kill him if he found out he'd bedded his little sister. And with his first race only days away, the timing couldn't have been worse. What? Was he trying to sabotage his newfound career?

"Mmm," he heard Marley murmur. Warm hands slipped beneath his arms, the front of Marley's body pressed up against his back.

He had to stop this.

If one of them didn't do something quick, trouble lay ahead.

He heard the rustling of the sheets and then the words, "Oh my gosh," all but a moan.

When he rolled onto his back and looked up at her, she was clutching her loose hair. "What have we done?" she groaned. She caught him staring at her and immediately jerked the covers up around her midsection.

"Marley—"

"We have to go," she said, her eyes darting around the room. "We're due back in the shop by noon. What time is it?" She turned toward the nightstand. "Nine o'clock! We were supposed to be out of here by eight!"

"Marley, calm down," he tried again.

She'd slipped from bed before he could stop her. "Get dressed."

"Whoa, whoa, whoa," he said. "Relax a little, would you? No one knows we're here."

"No one knows," she said. "No one knows," she repeated, jerking on her clothes. *"I know,"* she said.

"Yeah, but nobody else has to know."

"This is bad," he heard her murmur. "This is really bad. If Gil finds out…"

It didn't matter that he'd been thinking much the same thing not less than two minutes ago. Suddenly he felt on the defensive. "If Gil finds out, we'll deal with it."

"No," she said, her hands frozen on her skirt. "He can't find out."

"Why not?" Linc asked, sitting up on his elbows.

"Because he'll fire you."

"No, he won't."

"Then he'll fire me."

"Give me a break—"

"I promised him I'd stay away from you."

"You did *what?*"

She paused for a moment. "After everything that had happened between us, do you blame him for demanding I stay away from you?"

Well, when she put it that way…

"He said he needs you to focus on driving, not on me."

And he was right, Linc admitted.

"Of course, back then he was afraid I'd start stalking you again. He never anticipated… Never thought…" He saw her swallow. "I've got to go. My brother will be watching the clock, waiting for me to get back."

And Linc couldn't believe it. She was dumping him. Sure, she hadn't said the words, but he wasn't stupid. He knew where this conversation was headed.

"I want to have breakfast before we leave," he said.

"We'll get something on the way."

"I want a *good* breakfast."

"Good Lord," she said. "You can't be serious."

"I'm starving." He moved toward her. "Marley," he said again. "Calm down. Your brother's not going to think anything of us getting back to North Carolina late. He knows we bagged Shelter Home Improvement. We'll tell him we stayed up late to celebrate."

"He doesn't know," she said.

"You didn't call him?" Linc asked.

"When would I have done that? Before or *after* the second glass of champagne?"

She'd left her shirt partly undone and she looked sexy as hell standing there. Linc was half tempted to kiss her. Maybe that would stem the flow of words, but he sensed that would be a mistake.

"I'll call him and tell him."

"You will not," Marley said. "He can't know we're together."

"I'm not going to tell him that," Linc all but cried, running a hand through his hair. Damn it. He could still taste her, wanted to kiss her all over again.

"Nobody can know about this," she said. "And it can *never* happen again."

There they were—the words he'd been expecting. "So that's it? Wham, bam, thank you, ma'am? You're just going to use me and lose me?"

"That's exactly what I'm going to do…what I've done," she swiftly corrected, stuffing her belongings into her suitcase.

He couldn't believe it. Sure, he'd been expecting her to say that, but it still stung. Usually *he* was the one who broke up with a woman. "And you expect me to just walk away?"

"Of course," she said, picking up her purse and depositing it next to her briefcase on the credenza. "Isn't that what you normally do?"

"Well…" It was. He couldn't deny it. He'd never had a serious relationship in his life. He'd been too busy driving race cars. And then the accident had happened. To be honest, there'd been many times while he'd been recovering when he'd asked himself why he hadn't found the time to settle down.

"Look," he said, realizing she had turned to stare at him. He was bare-chested, out of sorts and unable to think clearly for some reason. "Last night was incredible." And it had been. "Really, Marley, you can't deny that."

He saw her face soften, saw the look of pain that entered her eyes. "I know," she said. "It was for me, too. But we can't do this again, Linc, we really can't. You have a new car to drive. I have a job to do. A brother I answer to. I can't tell you how sorry I am to have to tell you this, but we've got to be realistic."

He moved in closer. "No, we don't."

She lifted her chin, those sweeping eyebrows of hers lowering in determination. "I'm not going to risk my job, your job and *my* relationship with my brother—not for someone who's known for their inability to commit to a woman."

"Hey," he said. "That's not fair. Maybe I've never met the right woman."

Her eyes clouded. She shook her head. "It's over, Linc. I'll meet you downstairs." She unfurled the handle of her suitcase and slipped out the door.

Over, he repeated in his head. "No, it's not," he muttered. Not if he had anything to say about it.

THE DRIVE back home was excruciating. Marley knew Linc was upset, and she didn't blame him. It had to have chaffed when she'd broken up with him.

Broken up with him before it'd even began.

That was the saddest thing of all. For years she'd dreamed about being with Linc. Now that she'd finally managed to snag his attention, she couldn't see past her professional and family obligations to have a relationship with him.

Linc drove like a maniac the whole way back. The entire time he tried to persuade her to his way of thinking. She held firm. She told herself that he would thank her one day. That she wasn't cut out to be the girlfriend of a NASCAR driver. Especially one whose focus should be on relaunching his career. That's where her brother would want Linc's focus to be, too. After everything Gil had done for her in the past, she owed it to her brother to help his newest driver accomplish that goal.

"Thanks for driving," she told him as they pulled into Double S Racing's parking lot.

"No problem," he said, his jaw tense.

"I'll see you at the track this weekend?"

"I guess so."

He was furious. She told herself he'd get over it. She knew he had appointments this afternoon with his car chief and her brother. They'd called Gil on their way back to North Carolina. Gil had been overjoyed to learn she'd signed Shelter Home Improvement. He hadn't sounded the least bit suspicious, either, about their late departure. That had been a relief.

"See ya around, Martian Girl," Linc said, opening the driver's side door. Marley didn't immediately follow. But as she sat there she could admit to herself that she was devastated it had ended this way.

It's your own darn fault.

She'd wanted to play with fire and, look, she'd been burned. But she'd get over it quickly. They'd spent one night together. One flippin' night. Sure, it'd been amazing. She closed her eyes, allowed herself a moment to recall the way his mouth had felt against her own, how just the touch of his hands could make her sigh…how the look in his eyes could melt her heart.

"Damn it," she muttered, surprised to note tears in her eyes. "Get a grip, Marley."

She was doing the right thing. It might not seem like it now, but one day they would both look back and be grateful for her sensible actions.

She just wished she really believed that.

MARLEY SPENT the rest of the week doing everything she could to avoid Linc. It wasn't all that hard. Finalizing the deal between Double S Racing and Shelter Home Improvement took every moment of her time. Contracts needed to be drawn, but because there was a race this weekend—and Sharon wanted her company's name on the hood of Linc's car—they'd had to expedite matters. That meant trips to their corporate attorney's office, late hours at the office as she reviewed his recommended legal clauses, more trips to the attorney's office—and faxing. Lots and lots of faxing. It was almost a surprise to learn that it was Friday and Sharon expected to be at the track tomorrow. Apparently, she had no idea how difficult it was to secure Hot Passes.

"Okay," Emma-Lee said, bursting into her office late Friday afternoon. "I have you on a late-night flight to Kansas City. You'll leave at eight p.m."

Great, Marley thought.

"Sorry, but that was the best I could do on such short notice. Ms. Taylor will be taking the corporate jet and so she'll be there first thing Saturday morning and she wanted *you* there to greet her. Rhonda in the credential office has promised me she'd have everything covered for all the Shelter Home Improvement VIPs, but if you need anything—"

Emma-Lee didn't need to finish. The woman was always the epitome of efficiency.

"Thanks, Emma-Lee," Marley said.

"You're welcome, but I'm leaving for the day. Whew. I'm beat."

So was Marley. She didn't know how she'd make it to the airport on time what with everything she still had to do, but that was the nature of the NASCAR beast. It was a crazy lifestyle when one followed the circuit, one she didn't really want for herself. She preferred to stay at home. To enjoy her weekends relaxing. She rarely flew to the track once the sponsors were on board, but things had happened so quickly with Shelter Home Improvement that she really had no choice. Sharon needed to meet their public relations manager for Linc, the associate sponsors, Linc's team…the list went on, and Gil had asked her to make the introductions.

And so she forced herself aboard the commercial flight. Marley was never more relieved than when she fell into her hotel room bed near midnight.

She dreamed of Linc.

They were back at The Plantation and he was kissing her, only something kept buzzing near her ear and the sound was an annoyance….

She woke up with a start.

The alarm she had set was going off. That was the buzzing noise she heard. But she still had goose bumps from her dream, could still perfectly recall the way it'd felt to have Linc's lips traipsing up her belly and toward—

She groaned, clutched her head, then forced herself out of bed.

What she needed was a cold shower.

CHAPTER SEVEN

THE TRACK was every bit as crazy as she'd thought it would be. Since it was Saturday, race traffic wasn't horrible, and she left early enough that she didn't have to worry about a rush of people clogging up the entrances. Still, it took her a moment to find a parking spot in front of the white credential trailer. Cars came and went inside the enclosed area. Sharon was right outside the entrance, looking crisp and professional in her tan slacks and Shelter Home Improvement polo shirt that was the same green as their logo.

"These are for Linc," she said, handing Marley a bundle of the same shirts.

"Thanks," Marley said. Linc's PR representative had been asking for the shirts from the moment they'd agreed to the sponsorship deal.

"Marley," Sharon said, "this is Tim Atkinson, he's our CFO. Brett Miller, our COO…"

Marley tried to pay attention. She was usually pretty good at matching faces with names, but for some reason she found it hard to focus. "Why don't you follow me inside," she said. "You can fill out your forms in there."

The track at Kansas was situated out in the middle of a vast plain—but so was most of Kansas, Marley thought. In any event, wind was frequently a factor and today was no exception. The warm October breeze smacked her in the face as she led the Shelter Home Improvement group inside. Given the number of people she had to check in, NASCAR processed their paperwork in record time and so it was only a matter of minutes before Marley was waiting for Sharon and company to hop into their car so they could follow her into the infield.

Where she would see Linc.

Her stomach felt like a Chinese knot all of a sudden. Her mouth went dry. Her palms began to sweat. What would she say to him? she thought as she passed through the infield tunnel. How would he act toward her? She hadn't heard from him since they'd said goodbye in the Double S parking lot, not that she was surprised. She'd made it clear on the ride home that their "affair" was over.

Brenda, Linc's PR rep, greeted them outside the garage area, Marley performing the introductions. She was never more relieved than when she handed over control of the group to Brenda, explaining to Sharon that she had some things to do while Brenda took them on tour. Before she trotted off, Brenda handed her a sheet of paper.

"Linc's itinerary today," she said.

Marley swallowed, but she waited until the group walked away before glancing down at the piece of paper.

Interview with KBNT @ station—12:00 p.m.

Marley's shoulders relaxed. He wasn't even at the track. Not yet, at least. He was due to return in a couple hours, in time for the final practice session, but now that she had his schedule, she could avoid him all day. All she had to do was make sure she was far away from wherever he was.

Simple.

That's exactly how it worked out, too. She ran around the track without fear of bumping into him. She even finagled her way out of the Shelter Home Improvement sponsor party that night, pleading exhaustion. Everyone knew how hard she'd worked to get the i's dotted and the t's crossed before this weekend's race, so nobody batted an eye. Gil was there to take the lead.

Race day would be different. She knew that. Dreaded that. Fell into a restless sleep because of what she knew she'd go through tomorrow.

It wouldn't be fun.

IN SPITE of a few unique characteristics, Kansas looked a lot like a number of race tracks on the circuit. The layout was familiar—garages on the frontstretch, infield parking along the back. Even the grandstands looked the same as other tracks. Massive steel and aluminum girders held together stands that would seat thousands of fans. Those seats were mostly empty when she showed up early in the morning, but she knew they would quickly fill up the closer the time approached noon.

Of course, there would be no avoiding Linc that day. Sure enough, first person she ran into was the person she hoped most to avoid.

He was standing outside the hauler in his civies (as Marley liked to call them), his civilian clothes. Still, he was instantly recognizable. Nothing illustrated that better than the crowd of race fans that hung back from him as he talked to Bob Danson, his crew chief. They must have been discussing the handling of the car because Linc was using his fingers to demonstrate what his car was doing as it rounded a corner—or so it looked to Marley. She ducked her head and hoped he hadn't noticed her.

She should have known better.

"Marley, I need to talk to you."

Marley nodded a greeting to his crew chief before saying, "What about?" in what she hoped was a chipper-sounding voice.

"In private," he added.

She glanced at Bob again. The crew chief stared at her blankly. "I'll see what I can do about that problem during the first pit stop," Bob said.

"Thanks," Linc said before focusing his attention on her—but not before half a dozen fans came up to him and begged for an autograph. And here was all the proof Marley needed. Mixed into that crowd were several stunningly beautiful women. For a moment she wondered if they were all together, but they weren't. Two were with dates…or husbands. One appeared to be by herself. Apparently, fans hadn't forgotten about him. Good for Linc.

But it was hard to watch those women smile up at Linc as if they hoped he'd give them more than his autograph. Yes, even the married ones.

And that's exactly why you shouldn't date Linc. Even if you overcame your own moral obligations to your brother, there was still this to deal with. Still the fact that he was famous and you'd always have to play second fiddle to the first love of his life: racing.

"Why don't I catch up to you later?" she asked.

"No," he instantly contradicted, his gaze on the piece of paper he signed. "I'll be done here in a second if you just hold on."

"Good to see you back," one of the fans—an older, gray-haired man wearing sunglasses said. He wore a red-and-white Linc Shepherd shirt…one from the old days. "How's the leg?"

"Good," Linc said, his pen moving across the photograph the man held. He turned without ever really meeting the man's eyes to sign something else.

"Can't wait to see you in Victory Lane," another person said.

They loved him. Marley could understand why. The former NASCAR Sprint Cup Series champion had a winning smile and an easy way. She knew first-hand the power of that smile—had fallen in love with it when she was younger.

Love?

She shied away from the thought. She'd been too young to know what love was.

And now…

"Over here," Linc said, drawing her toward the back of the hauler. It was cooler beneath the shadow of the car lift that hung like a swinging garage door above their heads. She caught a glimpse of herself in the reflective surface of the sliding glass doors. She wore one of the new Shelter Home Improvement shirts, and the color didn't suit her skin. She looked pale. Of course, that could just be stress.

"I'm going to call you next week so we can schedule a date."

She drew back in shock. "What?"

"This is stupid, Marley. I don't know about you, but I can't stop thinking about the other night—"

"Linc—"

"Shh," he said. "Let me finish. I know there's a few obstacles to overcome…"

A few? she wanted to ask.

"But we're two mature adults. We can work it out."

Marley looked up. Gil, a commanding figure in the garage, was walking toward them. He was only in his early forties, but he wore power like an invisible suit. Heads turned as he walked by, and not just because he was as recognizable as his drivers. No. It was his fit body and his purposeful stride. He walked up to them.

"Hey, Linc," he said with a nod.

"Gil," he said.

And therein lie the crux of the problem. Her brother was Linc's boss. If he caught wind of their affair, she couldn't imagine he'd be pleased. She'd made a fool of herself over Linc once before. Her brother would worry that she'd do something rash yet again…and maybe he'd be right. Gosh. She didn't know what to think.

"Marley," her brother said, a smile coming over his face.

"Hey, you," she said with an answering grin.

"Thanks for sticking around this weekend."

"You're welcome." She'd rather be at home.

"Are you feeling good about today?" her brother asked his new star driver.

"You bet," Linc said with a wide smile.

"Good," Gil said with a nod. "How's the leg holding up?"

Marley could tell the question bothered Linc. He was

probably tired of people mentioning it. "Feels fine," he said.

"Then I expect you to win."

"Gonna try," he said.

"You going to watch the race from pit road or our suite?" Gil asked her.

Marley instantly shook her head. "I'm going to head back to the hotel."

She caught Linc staring at her.

"Right now," she added.

"Now?" Gil asked, surprised.

"I'm tired, Gil," she said. "And there's really no need for me to stay." But she was talking to Linc, and he knew it. "Brenda has things under control with the Shelter Home Improvement people, and I need to catch up on some sleep. If I leave early, I might actually get home in time to get some rest."

Her brother nodded, concern clouding his eyes. "No problem," he said. "But you're going to miss Linc's big debut."

"I know," she said. "But he'll do fine."

When she dared to meet Linc's gaze, it was clear he wasn't happy. Gil stared between the two of them, his frown causing lines to form above his brows. "Call me when you get home."

Did he sense something between them? Her brother was no fool, and he'd known her for her entire life. Just the other day he'd reminded her of the raging crush she'd had on Linc all those years ago. That car she'd set on fire had *not* been one of her better teenage moments.

"'Bye, Linc," Marley said, trying to throw her brother off the scent. "Be safe this afternoon."

"Marley," he said.

But she walked away before he gave the game away.

I'm going to call you later this week.

Would he? And what would she do if he did?

CHAPTER EIGHT

SHE WATCHED the race from the airport while waiting standby for the next flight home. Part of that race, anyway. She missed the last half and so it wasn't until she landed that she learned Linc had finished fourteenth.

Not bad.

She was happy for him. And even happier for her brother. She just hoped Linc didn't do as he threatened and call her that week.

He did something worse.

He dropped by her office. "We need to talk," he said, slamming her door closed.

"Congratulations on a great finish," she said.

"Fourteenth is *not* a great finish," he said, advancing toward her.

She sat behind her desk, but she felt like a lion tamer in the middle of a circus ring, and this feral animal had her firmly in his sights.

"Linc—"

"Quiet," he said.

"I beg your par—"

He jerked her to him. She gasped, used her body as a counterweight. He managed to get her out of her chair just the same, the plastic seat spinning out from under her.

"Don't," she told him.

"Sorry. I can't seem to help myself," he said, just before he lowered his head.

Her whole body had come alive. Her lips tingled in anticipation. Her breath caught.

It was just as she remembered.

She'd wondered if their night together had been an illusion, if the fact that she'd had a couple glasses of champagne had clouded her perception. It hadn't. If anything, it'd dulled it because kissing Linc in her office was better that morning than it'd been in the hotel room.

Because she knew what he could do to her.

She remembered every exquisite way he'd elicited pleasure. Felt her whole body curve into him in anticipation. She wanted those feelings again, wanted to know the touch of his hands, the feel of his lips against the sensitive skin near her belly.

"No," she moaned, pulling back. Dear God, what if her brother walked in? "Linc, no," she said when it appeared as if he was coming back for more.

"We're not going to fight this, Marley."

"Yes, we are," she said. "Damn it, Linc. This is madness."

"You want to know what's crazy?" he asked. "What's crazy is that yesterday was my first day back in a race car in years, and I did well. But the joy I felt at placing fourteenth ran a distant second to how I felt in your arms."

She couldn't breathe for a moment, felt her resolve weakening.

"Spend the day with me," he said.

"Linc, you know I can't. I have work to do. And I left the track early yesterday. If I do something rash, like leave with you on my arm, my brother will surely hear about it."

"So?"

She shook her head. "I can't."

"We can," he said. "Meet me for lunch, then. We'll call it business."

She was tempted. Oh, how she was tempted. But she just couldn't see her way past all the obstacles. She'd promised Gil. Darn it, she owed it to her brother to stay away from his star driver, at least while he was trying to make his big comeback.

"I'm not taking no for an answer, but if it'll make you feel any better, I'll call Emma-Lee and have her arrange it. That way, it'll look more official. We can discuss business."

No, she couldn't. She really, really shouldn't.

But she wanted to. She remembered what it felt like to have his mouth cover hers. She'd fantasized about what it would be like to be kissed by him for too many years to walk away from him now. She tried to remain strong, to keep resisting him, but the look in his gray eyes was her undoing. They burned into her own…taunting her, challenging her, reminding her.

"Okay, fine," she said.

Because if she were honest with hèrself, she'd never really stood a chance.

THEY NEVER MADE IT to the restaurant. Linc stopped on the side of the road—the two of them having left in separate cars—and asked if she'd rather eat lunch at his house. Of course, she knew what he was really asking, and all it took was one look into his heated eyes to convince her to follow him.

She was such a fool.

It was like playing with fire. For a moment she wondered if that wasn't part of the allure. He was forbidden. Off limits. Someone she should avoid at all cost, but she'd always had a thing for Linc and so maybe that wasn't it at all.

Linc's home was in the opposite direction of most of the NASCAR community. It was still off Davidson Highway, but east of most of the race shops. As she pulled between the brick pillars that guarded the entrance to his home, she found herself thinking racing had been good to him. Nothing illustrated that better than the home he lived in. It appeared to be one story, but it sprawled along the top of a hill overlooking a green valley. Secluded, sheltered and set back from the road, it was like a seashell set atop a beach, especially with the granite rocks that framed the lower third of its walls. Windows peeked out, scores of them, all at different angles. The exterior was painted a soft pink that should have looked out of place in the south, but that somehow worked in this setting. Billowy clouds hung overhead, causing the valley below to be dotted by gray shadows.

"It's beautiful," she said, slipping from her car.

"I know," he said, but he wasn't looking at the house, he was looking at her.

Marley knew they wouldn't be eating lunch then, especially when he kissed her. That was all it took—just one touch and food was the furthest thing from her mind. His mind, too, it seemed.

"Let's go inside," he said, drawing back and holding out his hand.

They walked, hand in hand, toward his home.

SHE AGREED to a secret affair. That way, if things didn't work out, her brother would never know about it and she wouldn't have to live her life hearing his "I told you so" over and over again. And so they became coworkers in the office by day, lovers by night.

"You've certainly got a glow about you," her brother said, popping his head into her office.

It was the Monday after the California race, her brother completely oblivious to the fact that Marley had flown in to be with Linc before and after the race. It was a simple matter to get there via a commercial flight. Simpler still to keep to herself in Linc's motor home. As it turned out, it was a good thing she'd made the trip. Linc had wrecked early in the race. He'd managed to limp home in second-to-last place and so, fortunately, Marley had been around to distract him.

"Maybe I'm pregnant," Marley quipped, not because she was serious—they were taking precautions—but because she enjoyed the momentary look of horror on her brother's face.

"You're kidding, right?" he asked, his blue eyes widening.

Marley shook her head. "When would I have time to get pregnant?" she asked.

Gil's face immediately softened.

"Besides, you need to be dating someone before you can get pregnant."

It was a blatant attempt to throw him off target, and it worked. "You're right," he said. "You really don't have much of a social life." He cocked his head sideways. "Why is that?"

"Because you keep me too busy for that."

He stared at her, a perplexed look on his face. "Do I?" he asked.

"You do," she said. "But I guess that's partly my fault. I could back off my work schedule if I got serious about a guy." It was the perfect opportunity to feel Gil out, to see if he'd mind her dating Linc and so she said, "How would you feel about me dating someone in the industry?"

"Are you?" he asked.

She nibbled her lip for a moment.

"No," she said quickly. "Of course not. I hardly have the time."

But she hated…she absolutely *hated* to lie.

"So this is a hypothetical question?" he asked.

She nodded.

"I guess it depends on the man. And if I thought he was good enough for you."

She smiled weakly. Would he think Linc was good enough for her? He'd hired him as a driver and so he must respect him on some level. She almost told him then…almost. Something held her back because deep down inside there was a part of her that worried…what if it didn't work out? What if she told her brother everything and in the end Linc broke her heart? And God forbid their mother ever find out. It was bad enough Marley actually worked for a living…at least in her mother's eyes. Heaven help them all if Marley dated a grease monkey. That's how her mother would see Linc, no matter his actual job. What would happen when the truth came out?

She didn't want to find out.

"Then I guess I'll have to pick the right man," she said absently.

She had a feeling her brother knew something was afoot. Intelligent, highly educated, he didn't get to the top of the NASCAR game by being stupid. So she wasn't surprised when he came forward, rested his hands against the front of her desk. "If you have someone in mind," he said, "be careful, little sis. Some guys might want to use you to get close to me."

She drew back in surprise. Was that what Linc was doing? Was he using her to solidify his place at Double S Racing?

No.

That was ridiculous.

"You know how it is," he said. "Some men will do whatever they can to get to the top and so I'll be honest. If you dated someone within the NASCAR industry, it'd have to be someone pretty high up. Someone already well established."

Marley gulped. She didn't live with her head in the sand by any means. She was trying to be realistic where Linc was concerned, but she just didn't see him as the type that would use her. Not like that. Maybe that was naive, but she'd like to think she was a good judge of character.

"Well then, you'll be relieved to know you have nothing to worry about." She almost added that she *wasn't* dating a driver, but she couldn't be that dishonest. "I duly promise to date only men at the top of the heap."

Still, Gil looked at her suspiciously. "Your choice," he said.

And it was. She just hoped it was the right choice.

A WEEK PASSED. Marley secretly accompanied Linc to yet another race, this one in Charlotte, and to be honest,

she was getting a little tired of it all. She lived in fear
that she'd bump into Gil. If things worked out between
her and Linc, she wanted to be the one to tell Gil. She
didn't want him to get the news second hand. And God
help her if her mother popped in for a visit.

But she had bigger fish to fry. Linc was in a slump.

Hard to imagine calling a man a failure after only
three races, but that's exactly what the media did. They
claimed he was washed up. That he had no business
being back in a race car. That he should hang up his
steering wheel and maybe try car ownership instead.

"I feel like doing exactly that," Linc said, despondent,
his face in deep shadows. It was near midnight, as the
mid-autumn race held had been at night. They stood
just outside his motor home. Beneath giant klieg lights,
Marley could see that the grandstands were slowly emp-
tying of race fans. It was a local race and so at least
Marley was close to home.

"Linc," she said softly, glancing around to ensure her
brother wasn't walking up to them. Even at this time of
night, the Drivers' and Owners' parking lot was well lit.
"Give it time. You know how it is with a new team."

"Yeah, but these days owners expect results right
away."

That was true, she thought, glancing around. The
parking area was a city unto itself. Even though the
race was close to home, most of the drivers and their
crew members kept motor homes nearby, as places
where they could rest and relax away from the garage
throughout the weekend. Buses and recreational vehicles covered every square inch of the blacktop. She
and Linc were relatively excluded. Still…her brother

could appear at any moment. He'd even parked his car near Linc's motor home.

"Gil's not like that," Marley said, growing more and more tense by the minute. She'd followed Linc back from the garage, but she knew time was short. The haulers would begin pulling out at any moment. Beyond the Drivers' and Owners' lot, she could hear a stream of cars and recreational vehicles leaving the track.

"I sure hope not," he said, staring off into the distance.

And Marley's heart broke for him. She could see such a mix of emotion on his face. Sadness. Resignation. *Fear.*

"Linc, it's okay," she said, reaching out and placing a hand on his arm. Damn it. She wanted to slip into his arms, to ease the ache in his eyes. But she couldn't. Not here. "Just focus on next week."

He nodded. "But that would be easier to do…with you by my side."

"I *am* by your side," she said.

"Not like I want you to be."

She knew what he meant, glanced around to make sure they were alone before stepping closer. More than a few people were returning from the garage. A few buses down, one of the diesel engines revved to life. Before long, team members would start to roll out, some in regular vehicles, others in their motor home. They didn't have much time.

"Give it a few weeks," Marley said. A few weeks for her to decide if this would all shake out. "Talk to Gil tomorrow. Explain how hard you're trying. I'm sure he'll understand."

He nodded, looked off into the distance. She knew he

was thinking about the race he'd just run. He'd finished thirty-ninth. Awful…especially for a man used to being on top, it was hell to find himself at the bottom of the score board.

"I just hate to think he might believe I've lost my touch."

And this was the hard part of the business, the part most magazines and e-zines didn't talk about. How demoralizing it was to the drivers who weren't performing well. How even the most talented driver could be reduced to an insecure mess. But most of all, how a driver would beat himself up when he wasn't driving up to an owner's standards. Linc's situation was complicated by that plane crash. The tragic accident had taken more than the lives of his friends.

"Look," she said, scooting as close to him as she dared. "No driver is fired less than a month after being hired. You know that and I know that. Don't stress. My brother's not going to let you go just because of a few bad finishes. I won't let him."

His eyes never left hers. She saw him shift, felt his hand caress the side of her cheek. "Thank God I have you."

She leaned her face into him. "See what happens when you get me drunk?"

"You weren't drunk," he said with a laugh. Marley was glad to hear it. "You were tipsy."

She smiled. "Ah, yes, tipsy," she said, wishing he would go on touching her all night. But it was already late, and she had an early morning meeting. As much as she'd love to spend the night in his arms, it wasn't feasible.

"I better get going," she said.

"Not yet," he replied softly.

She knew what he was going to do before he did it; she could see the intent in his eyes. And just seeing that spark, knowing that was sexual interest that simmered in his eyes—it caused her own body to ignite. So she didn't draw away. She would be a fool to do so. Somehow, remarkably, she'd managed to capture the attention of this amazing man. If she were honest with herself, there was a part of her that wanted the world to know it.

Her eyes closed of their own volition. She could feel every soft curve of his lips, the pressure of his mouth increasing with every second that passed. She knew what he wanted, resisted opening her mouth. If she did that, she'd lose all sense of reason. She couldn't allow that to happen, not with Gil so close—

His tongue swiped her lower lip.

She moaned. He took advantage of her slightly open mouth. His tongue was warm, and he tasted of coffee and mints. She touched him back, lifted her hands to his chest, not to push him away, but to feel the beat of his heart beneath his shirt. She loved kissing him. Loved touching him even more. There was a part of her— even now—that still couldn't believe she was with Linc Shepherd. And so what would it hurt if she let him kiss her for a minute…just a minute—

"What in the *hell* are you doing?"

They both drew apart, and it didn't take bright lights to see that her brother was stunned to find her in Linc's arms. Worse, he was hurt. She could see how betrayed he felt in his eyes.

CHAPTER NINE

"GIL," LINC SAID, tugging Marley to his side. "I know this looks bad."

"You lied to me," he said, staring at Marley.

"No. Not really. I mean, I told you I was thinking of dating someone in the industry—"

"But Linc Shepherd?" He ran a hand through his hair. "I can't believe you meant Linc."

"We've been dating for weeks," Linc felt the need to point out.

It was the wrong thing to say to his boss. Linc felt Marley tense alongside of him.

"Is this true?" Gil asked.

Linc glanced down in time to watch Marley nod miserably. "It is," she said.

And then Gil's bewildered gaze snagged Linc's. "And you went along with her?"

"He didn't 'go along' with me."

"You mean he made the first pass?" Gil asked.

Linc saw Marley look away again.

Gil glared at him next. "I hired you to drive cars, not hop into bed with my sister."

"Gil!" Marley cried.

The words stung, Linc's guilt compounded by the realization that his boss had a point. He should have been focusing on driving, not Marley. This was his shot at a comeback and look at what a mess he'd made of it.

"Is this why your finishes have dropped off?" Gil asked.

"No," Linc said.

But was it? Was Marley the reason why he was so unfocused? Was he shooting himself in the foot careerwise…over a woman? He scrubbed a hand over his face.

"Really," Gil said, looking between the two of them. "I wonder."

Linc wondered, too.

"You hurt me, Marley," Gil said, his eyes filled with sadness. "You should have been honest with me the other day."

"I know," she said, meeting her brother's gaze head-on. "But I didn't want to worry you."

"So you snuck around behind my back."

Neither of them said a word. "I'm disappointed in both of you," Gil said before turning and walking off.

"Gil," Marley said, stepping away from him.

But her brother was already gone. Marley tried to follow, Linc held her back. "Give him a few hours."

"He's devastated. It's going to take him longer than that," Marley said, worry creasing her forehead.

"No, it's not."

"I've never lied to him before."

"You had your reasons," he said.

She met his gaze. "Did I?"

He touched her face, gently turned her toward him. "He'll get over it. You're his baby sister," he said gently.

She nodded, her eyes sad. "I know."

"But I don't think of you as a kid anymore."

Her face softened a bit. "I sure hope not."

And it was good to know he could kiss her now, really, truly kiss her. But when his lips lowered to hers, she didn't immediately respond. She was stiff in his arms, too.

"What's wrong?" he asked.

She shook her head a bit. "I'm just sorry Gil had to find out this way."

"It was bound to happen sooner or later."

She nodded. "Maybe we should cool things off for a bit."

"No," he said. "If we do that, it'll look even worse. Like we weren't really serious about each other or something."

"You think?"

"I know," he said firmly.

"You're probably right, but I should still get going," she said. "If I'm not at work on time tomorrow, I'm sure Gil will know. He'll be keeping close tabs on me now."

Linc released her, though he hated to do so. To be honest, he'd become more and more dependent on her in recent weeks. Not a day went by, sometimes not even hours, when he wasn't talking to her. It amazed him that the bothersome teenage girl had grown into such a complex, fascinating woman.

He refused to give her up. Refused.

"Okay," he said, giving her a small peck on the lips. "I'll call you in the morning."

She nodded. But as she walked away, and the drama of the night wore off, he began to wonder if she wasn't right. Gil had every reason to feel betrayed. The man had put faith in Linc's abilities when no one else would. And what had he done? Linc had slept with his sister, behind the man's back no less.

"Damn," he muttered. He'd have to go apologize.

And pray to God he didn't get fired.

MARLEY DREADED going into work the next morning.

"Gil would like to see you," Emma-Lee said, pouncing on her in the hallway.

It wasn't even eight o'clock yet. Marley had come in early. To be honest, she'd been hoping to get to work ahead of her brother so she wouldn't bump into him in the parking lot.

Oh, well.

"Okay, thanks," she said.

"What'd you do?" Emma-Lee said, her blue eyes full of curiosity. "He doesn't look happy."

Marley shook her head. "Nothing."

Gil's offices were on the second floor, too, and so as she walked up the steps near the main reception area, her feet felt leaden. She didn't know what he would say to her, but she had a feeling it wouldn't be good. Despite the fact that she was a grown woman, Gil was still her older brother. She felt a lecture coming on.

She knocked on his door lightly, popping her head in before he could answer. "You wanted to see me?" she asked.

He sat behind a large desk—"the throne," she'd dubbed it—with a window behind him. His office was done in shades of gray; the desk he sat behind made of glass and chrome. He had his chair turned away from the door. Marley realized that he'd watched her cross the parking lot. Terrific.

"Gil?" she said when he didn't immediately turn around. Her mind was filled with trepidation as she entered his office. Slowly, he turned to face her.

The look on his face was enough to make her flinch.

"Sit down," he said, motioning to one of two chairs in front of his desk.

She didn't want to. She really didn't. Suddenly, she felt about ten years old. "Gil, about last night—"

He held up a hand. She instantly quieted.

"Marley, how many years have you worked for me now?"

Marley gulped, had to wrack her brains for a moment or two. "Since college," she said. "About seven years now, I guess."

He nodded, and she had to admit, he looked every inch the big brother sitting there. Face grave. Eyes serious. Back straight. "And have I ever asked you to do something you don't want to do?"

She could tell he'd stayed up all night thinking about what he wanted to say to her. "No," she said.

"And don't I always have your best interest at heart?"

"Yes," she said, sinking into her chair.

"Then break things off with Linc."

"No."

Gil leaned forward, made a temple out of his hands and tapped them against his mouth. She knew the gesture well. He was trying to formulate his words. He'd done the same thing after she'd set Linc's car on fire.

And she *still* couldn't believe she'd done that.

"I don't want you dating him," he said.

She opened her mouth to protest.

"But not for the reason you might think," he said. "I'm going to trust that you know what you're doing."

She relaxed.

"But this is bad timing. Linc's trying to make a come-back, and despite what you say, I'm not convinced you're not the reason why he's been off his game."

She gulped. Was her brother right? If she'd been honest with herself, that same fear had kept her up half the night.

"Gil—"

"Please, Marley."

The fight drained out of her. "I'll think about it," she said. But deep inside she wondered: What if she really *was* the problem? What then? What if, later on, Linc came to the same conclusion? What if he blamed her for his failed comeback?

Dear God, she didn't think she could take that.

"Just don't ask me to do anything right away," she said, holding up a hand when it appeared as if her brother would say something else. "I need some time."

He seemed to accept that.

Her shoulders were as heavy as anvils when she turned away. She knew what she had to do. Deep inside, she knew. She just hoped she had the courage to go through with it.

"What did he say?"

Linc knew he'd surprised her by the way she jumped. Her hand was to her chest as she turned to face him. "Linc. What are you doing here?"

"What do you mean what am I doing here?" he asked. "I work here."

They were in the hallway, not far from her office.

Linc glanced inside a nearby office. It belonged to somebody in marketing, judging by the nameplate on the outside wall. He ducked into it, hoping the office's owner didn't come into work early.

"What are you doing?" she asked.

He'd expected her to follow him, and when she didn't, hooked an arm through hers. "I want to talk to you."

"We can go into my office," she said, digging in her two-inch heels. She was dressed in her usual uniform. Black suit, light blue shirt beneath, hair swept back in a ponytail.

"Not if your brother might track you down there."

He could tell she wanted to tell him that Gil wouldn't do that, but they both knew he might walk down that hall at any moment. She shut the door.

"So?" he prompted.

She glanced over her shoulder, as if worried the owner of the office—or her brother—might burst in on them. "He asked me to break things off with you."

Linc couldn't keep the disappointment from his face, and he was certain she could see it. "You're not going to listen to him, are you?"

"I think I should," she said.

"Why?"

"Because I think he's right. I think I might be the reason you're in a slump. I think I owe it to my brother to back off and see. I think taking a breather might be good for us. Everything happened so fast."

He came forward. "You are not the reason why I'm performing so miserably," he said, clasping her shoulders with his hands.

She shook her head, her teeth working her lower lip as if she didn't trust herself to speak. When he saw her chin jut out, he almost groaned. "Are you sure of that? Can you honestly say you haven't felt the tiniest bit guilty about sleeping with the boss's sister?"

Her arrow hit the mark.

"You have, haven't you?"

"Only because I hated sneaking around behind your brother's back."

"I know. Me, too."

"We don't have to anymore." But he could tell by the look in her eyes that she wasn't going to listen to him.

"One of us has to be sensible," she said. "You've got so much riding on this. So does my brother. We all have a lot at stake. I've spent years and years watching my brother build this team. I'd hate to be responsible for taking it down."

"Marley," he said, "that's not going to happen."

"Do you love me, Linc?"

He drew back in surprise. "Of course I care for you. You know that."

"Enough to forgive me if it turns out my brother was right? If looking back on things two, three, four years from now you think to yourself, maybe she was right? Maybe I should have focused a little harder?"

"That's not what I would think."

She shook her head. "But I suppose in the end it doesn't matter. I can't risk it. I can't let my brother down. I can't let *you* down. I can't let the employees of Double S Racing down. Not for a few hours of pleasure."

"We have more going for us than lust. I care for you."

"Enough to stick by my side for the rest of our lives?"

He scrubbed a hand over his face.

"Really, Linc?"

He had no answer. He heard himself ask, "Are you saying *you* love me?"

She looked away, nibbled her lips some more. "To be honest, I think I've loved you since I was seventeen."

He felt his heart drop. "Marley—"

She was backing out of the office. "Goodbye, Linc."

"Marley, no—"

"This was a mistake," he heard her say.

"Damn it, it's not a mistake."

"Stay away from me, Linc. You'll see. This is for the best."

Two seconds later, the door closed behind her. He slammed his fist against the wall. "Damn it," he yelled.

But his voice echoed through an empty office.

CHAPTER TEN

HE REFUSED to call her. Would not give her the satisfaction. Refused to chase after her.

"Crap," he found himself yelling when his helmet fell to the floor of the hauler with a crack that almost made it sound as if the darn thing had broken. He knew that wasn't possible.

"You sound like a man on the edge."

Linc looked up in surprise. PDQ's star driver stood near the glass doors. At six foot two the man was an inch taller than himself, but there the similarities ended. Bart Branch was blond with blue eyes. Women went crazy over him, not that Linc cared. Here was the man Linc had been hired to beat, but who seemed unstoppable lately. Linc wouldn't be surprised if he won the championship this year. And that was okay. He was one of Linc's closest friends, a man who'd stood by his side after his accident.

"What are you doing here?"

"Just thought I'd check up on you. You looked a little worn out this morning."

"Bad week," he said.

They were at Martinsville. The NASCAR Nationwide Series cars were practicing outside. Linc could hear the rhythmic drone of engines.

"Yeah, I heard that," Bart said.

Linc turned, helmet forgotten. "Heard what?"

Bart smiled a bit wryly. "About Marley."

And Linc could only stare. "How?" he asked. And then he recovered himself. "I mean, what's this about Marley?"

But Bart was shaking his head. "You ought to know better than most that there are no secrets in the garage. Someone overheard you talking to Gil at Charlotte when he caught you kissing his sister."

Charlotte. The night he'd lost Marley. Still, Linc thought about denying it, told himself to tell Bart that he was wrong.

"I can't believe I missed it. How long have you two been dating?" Bart asked.

Linc shook his head dismissively. "Not long." *Too short an amount of time to feel this broken up over the whole thing*, Linc privately added.

"But you obviously care for her."

Linc shrugged. "We've known each other for a long time."

Bart nodded, his curly hair looking like it belonged on a California surfer rather than a NASCAR driver. "Sometimes, though, you can be with someone their entire life and not really know them."

The words made Linc still. It was a well-known fact that Bart's father, Hilton Branch, had embezzled a fortune and then vanished. The scandal had been a couple of years ago, but Linc suspected as Bart got better with each race, it would be dredged up again. The media loved to dig up old bones.

"Boy, ain't that the truth," Linc said. After he'd gotten out of the hospital and it looked like his career was over, he couldn't believe how many of his so-called "friends" had disappeared from his life. It'd been a huge eye-opener to see who had cared for him personally, and who had been using him because he was Linc Shepherd, former NASCAR Sprint Cup Series champion.

"It can get tough," Bart said.

For the first time Linc noticed Bart appeared troubled, too. The two of them had been as good friends as possible, given they were competitors on the race track.

"You sound like your personal life is in shambles, too."

It was Bart's turn to look uncomfortable. Linc wondered if Bart would deny it, but his former rival surprised him when he said. "You don't know the half of it."

Linc turned, leaned against the counter that ran the length of the trailer, and crossed his arms. "You need to talk?"

Bart shook his head, as if he planned to keep matters to himself. But then he blurted, "My dad had a second family."

Linc straightened in shock. "Say *what?*"

Bart nodded, his tension appearing to ease. "I heard it from my sister, Penny. She found out after visiting my dad in jail. The son of a bitch even had a child with the woman."

"Holy—" Linc didn't know what else to say. If word got out about this…

"And she's missing."

"Wait, wait, wait," Linc said. "Your father had a secret family and one of his children is missing?"

"His *only* child with his mistress, wife…whatever you want to call her," Bart said. "The daughter he had with the woman is a toddler and we have no idea where she is."

Unbelievable, Linc thought.

Bart ran a hand through his hair, his face growing troubled again. "You think *you've* got problems," Bart said, and Linc could tell he was trying to make a joke. "If I sat down and told you the whole sordid tale, it'd turn your hair gray."

Linc knew he could say something pithy, but his accident had taught him that sometimes people needed a sounding board.

"What are you going to do?" he asked.

"Find my half sister. Focus on the Chase. Keep this out of the media."

"Yeah, but if the press gets word of this—"

"Then I'll be front page news…again," Bart said with a wry twist of his lips. "Doesn't matter. I have to do what's right, and it doesn't sit well with me that somewhere out there I have a half sister that's God knows where living who knows what kind of life. My father might be a jerk, but I'm not."

Linc simply marveled. Here was a man who lived by his convictions. Who wasn't afraid to tempt fate to do what was right. Who didn't care what the consequences were as long as he could look himself in the mirror.

Despite nearly losing his life, Linc had never seen things in such clear shades of black and white.

But he had started to now.

"Anyway," Bart said, "my life is in shambles. How's yours?"

And it was funny. It was at that precise moment that Linc had a revelation. He was mad as hell about what had happened with Marley, but he had the power to change things…if he really, truly, honestly wanted to.

"You know," he said softly, "I think my life's going to turn out just fine."

"So you're okay with the fact that Marley's going to work for another company?"

"What?"

Bart looked as surprised by his outburst as Linc was. "You didn't know about it?"

"Start explaining. Now."

Bart's brows sank down. "Marley's brother found her another job. She's going to do PR for one of the associate sponsors."

"Like hell she will."

And for the first time Bart smiled. "So you *do* care for her."

Linc drew up in surprise.

"Don't bother denying it, Linc. I can tell by your eyes that you do."

Holy—

He was in love with her. How had that happened? When? Did she feel the same way, too?

Do you love me?

"You do, don't you?" Bart asked.

"I think I do," Linc admitted.

"Then go after her, man. Trust me. That's what it's all about. You more than anyone should know that. This—" he waved his hands. "Racing. It's all secondary to what's really important—family."

"I've been a fool," he said.

Bart laughed. "You got that right."

SHE WASN'T AT THE TRACK. Linc had known that. Still, he pulled off a top-ten finish. Frankly, he didn't care about how he did, and as he caught a flight home on Double S Racing's private plane, he recognized that that had been his problem his whole time.

He'd been trying too hard.

Once he'd decided that he didn't care about how he finished, he'd been set free.

She was leaving Double S Racing.

To hell she was.

He called Gil on his cell phone and demanded a private meeting. His new team owner hadn't been pleased when Linc had ordered him to appear at his office the next morning, but Linc hadn't cared. The man could fire him. In fact, he hoped he would. That would make things easier.

"Ah, Linc," the man said when Linc burst into his office without so much as a by-your-leave from Emma-Lee who sat behind a chrome-and-glass desk that matched Gil's.

"Gil," Linc said, resisting the urge to slam the door closed behind him. He couldn't have if he wanted to.

"Gil, I'm sorry," Emma-Lee said, the blonde somehow wedging herself between the door and its frame.

"It's okay," Gil said. "He has an appointment."

"He does?" Emma-Lee said, blue eyes widening.

"It's a private matter," Gil said. His gaze shifted to Linc's. "One we're going to resolve today…one way or the other."

Linc straightened, refusing to back down from the man. "Yes, we are," he said.

"Close the door, please, Emma-Lee."

The assistant did as ordered, but not before shooting the two of them a look of keen interest. Linc crossed to the front of Gil's desk once the door was closed. The glass top was cold when he placed his hands against it, leaning toward his boss. "I'm going to marry Marley."

He could tell they weren't the words Gil had been expecting because the man's eyes widened imperceptibly. "Are you, now?"

"I am," Linc said. "And I don't care if that means having to pay a small fortune to get out of my contract with you. I'm marrying your sister with or without your permission."

Gil leaned back in his chair, the thing squeaking as he did so. Linc straightened up slowly, crossing his arms in front of him as he waited for Gil's response.

"What makes you think you're good enough for her?" the man asked, blue eyes that were so like Marley's narrowing.

"I'm not," Linc said quickly. "She's the most sensitive, compassionate, intelligent woman I've ever met and I refuse to give her up."

And if he wasn't mistaken, he could have sworn the man's lips twitched a little…almost as if he'd just bit back a smile.

"You know," Gil said after a moment of tense silence, "twenty years ago I got into this business on a whim." He leaned forward slightly to pick up a pen. He fiddled with it absently as Linc stared down at him. "I never expected that my sister would want to follow me, but she did. At the time I promised my parents that I would keep an eye on her. They almost forbade her from ever visiting a race track again after the whole car fire debacle." He shook his head. "Things settled down once she went to college, and I was glad to see that she seemed to have gotten over her crush on you. But I'll be honest, Linc. I worried about you coming to work for us because of that crush. I was afraid she might embarrass herself all over again. Or that she might have grown to despise you over the years. I never, not once, expected the two of you to fall in love."

"It's the real deal, if that's what you're worried about."

"I guess it is."

"Oh, yeah?" Linc said. "Is that why you told her to find another job? So she could get over me? So she wouldn't have to deal with the pain of seeing me day in and day out? So that *you* wouldn't have to see the pain in her eyes?"

He'd hit a nerve, Linc could tell. He pressed his advantage in the same way he did out on the race track. "She loves me. I know it, and I'm going to go find her and tell her that now. So if you love your sister, you'll offer me your congratulations, wish me well and send me on my way."

No emotion flickered through Gil's eyes. Linc felt his pulse beat at the base of his neck as he waited for her brother's response.

"I'll expect your resignation on my desk by the end of the day."

"Why wait?" Linc said, fishing around in his pocket for an envelope. This was it. The moment of truth. He was about to give up racing for a chance at something bigger than him—his love for Marley.

"Here it is right now," he said firmly, though his voice was a near croak. He knew he was doing the right thing, but it still wasn't easy. "Have your lawyers contact mine about how much it's going to cost me to get out of my contract." He tossed the envelope on Gil's desk, his hands shaking. Linc watched the thing skate across the surface just before he turned away.

"She's not in her office," Gil called out as Linc clasped the handle. "She's down the street, at Power Productions, doing a photo shoot with Bart Branch."

Linc slowly turned to face the man.

"She's trying to learn a little something about PR before she leaves for her new job."

Linc held the man's gaze for a moment before saying, "Thank you."

The two of them studied each other for a moment. "Good luck," Gil ended up saying.

Linc felt a spurt of hope. Maybe, just maybe, there was hope.

"I'll need it," Linc said.

CHAPTER ELEVEN

IT WAS A SHORT DRIVE and Linc had never been more nervous in his life as he pulled to a stop in front of the single-story building. He'd known exactly where it was. Power Productions was well-known in the industry for their powerful driver promotions. They were one of the best in the business and if Bart was doing a photo shoot inside, it meant some serious publicity coming his way.

"Good morning," a bright-eyed receptionist said as he entered the building. "Can I help— Oh! Mr. Shepherd. How are you? We haven't seen you in a while."

Linc smiled, trying to set the woman at ease. He actually recognized the woman from some place. Wait. She'd worked the phones at one of his first race teams. "Lauren," he said. "How are you?"

"I'm fine," she said. The woman was older than him by about ten years, but this was a stroke of luck, Linc thought.

"Congratulations on hooking up with Double S Racing."

"Thanks," Linc said, trying not to wince. "Is Marley inside? I need to see her."

"Gil's sister? Yeah. She's with the production crew."

"Terrific," Linc said. "Is it okay if I go in?"

"Sure," the woman said. "Studio Five. You know the one. The big one at the end."

Linc nodded his thanks as the woman buzzed him through a private door. He did, indeed, know where it was. It had a roll-up door at one end so they could use a driver's car. "Thanks," Linc said before crossing through the door.

"My pleasure," Lauren said, Linc noticing that her blond hair had started to turn gray. Were they really getting that old?

Was he too old for Marley? he wondered as the door closed behind him. He was in a narrow hall, one with doors off to the left and right. He headed toward the room at the end.

To be honest he'd mulled over the question more times than he could count in the previous twenty-four hours. Did she have any interest in hooking up with a maybe washed up, forty-something-year-old driver? Did she love him?

He opened the door, his heart pounding as hard and as fast as it did on race day. Bart looked toward him as he swung the door wide. "Linc," he called out. "What the heck are you doing here, buddy?"

And there Marley was, standing off to the side, the look on her face one of dismay mixed with trepidation.

"I'm here to see Marley," Linc admitted.

Bart straightened a bit, then started to smile. He seemed to know which way the wind blew. "Good move," Bart said before turning to the right. "Time to take a break, folks. Let's clear out the studio."

"But we just got everything all set up," someone said. The photographer, Linc noticed, the man standing behind a fancy-looking camera on a tripod to his left. There were about four other people standing near him.

"Too bad," Bart said, walking toward a door. "I'm taking a break."

"But we just got the lighting right," the photographer whined. "Now we'll have to start all over again."

"Be back in five," Bart called.

"Bart," Marley said, trying to call him back.

But the driver didn't listen and reluctantly, everyone followed him out, although the photographer didn't look happy about it. Linc saw Marley start to leave, too, and raced forward to stop her.

"Stay," he ordered.

"Why?" she asked sharply.

"Because I'm in love with you."

She gasped and whispered, "Oh!" Her eyes filled with tears.

"And if I'm not mistaken," he said, gently lifting her chin, "you love me, too."

He saw her swallow, saw her blink back tears. "I do," she admitted softly.

He couldn't keep the grin from his face. "That's what I thought."

"But, Gil. Your job. If we start dating, my brother will throw a fit—"

"I resigned."

"You did *what?*"

"I quit."

"You can't do that."

He clasped her face between his hands. "Why? Are you the only one that's allowed to find another job?"

"Well, no," she admitted. "But if one of us has to quit, it should probably be me."

He couldn't wait any longer. He folded her in his arms, and as he did so, he realized it felt right…absolutely right. Bart had been right. This was what it was all about. Family. Connections. Being loved—and loving someone in return. His lips found hers, and if he had any doubts that she loved him, too, they evaporated beneath the heat of that kiss. He wanted to push her up against Bart's car, but he knew he couldn't do that. No. That could wait. For later.

"Marry me, Martian Girl?" he asked, pulling back.

He saw her lips twitch before she softly answered, "Yes," and then sank into his arms. "Yes, yes, yes," she muttered, hugging him tight.

"And you're not going to quit your job," he said, resting his chin on top of her head. "Your brother would hate me even more if I forced you to do that."

"I don't hate you."

They both drew apart. Gil stood in the entrance, the look on his face one Linc would never forget.

"I just needed to make sure you loved Marley more than anything else in life." He held up a letter. "And I have that proof right here."

He heard Marley gasp back a sob. "Gil," she said, her voice clogged with tears. "I'm so glad to see you. I feel so bad about everything that happened."

Her brother came forward, Marley sinking into his arms. "I promised our parents I'd look out for you, Marley. I needed to make sure he really loved you."

"He does," Marley answered.

"I know that now," Gil said, looking Linc in the eye.

"I do," he admitted.

"Good, because I can't have my future brother-in-law driving for me if he doesn't truly love my sister."

"Oh, Gil," Marley said, pulling back.

"Here," Gil said, handing Linc the envelope he'd slid across the man's desk less than a half hour ago. But Linc hesitated.

"Take it," Gil repeated.

"What if I've lost my touch?" Linc said, confessing his biggest fear to the both of them.

"Then we'll figure something out," Gil said. "But something tells me you'll do just fine."

He heard Marley sniff again, knew she was fighting back tears. Linc opened his arms. Marley sank into them. "Thank you," he mouthed to Gil over the top of her head.

Marley's brother had tears in his eyes, too. "You're welcome," he answered back.

As it turned out, Gil was right. He didn't do "just fine." Two years later, Linc won his third championship, and as Marley stood beside him in Victory Lane, paper pieces fluttering down around them, he knew they'd made the right choice all those years ago.

"I love you, Martian Girl," he whispered in her ear.

"I love you, too," she replied over the sound of the crowd.

They kissed, the crowd going wild all over again. Linc smiled to himself, knowing in that moment that he hadn't been given just a second chance, he'd been given a shot at a whole new life, one he couldn't imagine without Marley.

* * * * *

Talk to Me

Dorien Kelly

CHAPTER ONE

SUSIE EDMONDS found it a little scary that she was beginning to feel an emotional bond with her daughter's hamster. Both she and the hamster ran in endless circles, ultimately getting nowhere—the hamster on his wheel and Susie on her daily after-school route. The hamster, however, remained blessedly oblivious to the fact that his owner, fourteen-year-old Camille, had taken the hormonal plunge into adolescence. As a non-English speaker, the hamster couldn't discern between the standard sweet, agreeable Cammie or the diva-in-training who was taking over her body with increasing frequency. Sadly, Susie could.

"Mom, we need to pick up my new riding boots before Matt's soccer practice. If you drop him off first, there won't be time to get them and my life will be totally ruined," Cammie announced from her seat beside Susie in the family's SUV.

Susie did her best to hide a smile at her daughter's dire tone. The diva was most definitely in the house... or at least the vehicle. But it was a lovely early October Monday afternoon, with just a bit of cool to the North Carolina air, and Susie wasn't going to allow Cammie's mood to dim the sunshine.

"Sweetheart, I fail to see how getting Matt to practice on time is going to ruin your life," she said.

Susie glanced in the rearview mirror to see how ten-year-old Matt was holding up. Wise boy that he was, he'd tucked his earbuds in and was rocking away to the beat of his favorite band. He was so much his father's son, from the cleft in his chin right down to that wonderful "go with the flow" personality that Susie adored.

Cammie gave a drama queen sigh to accompany a toss of her brown ponytail. "I need to get those boots broken in before the show next Saturday. If I don't, it's going to be a disaster!"

"You can wear your old boots for the show."

"I'd die first!"

Susie gripped the steering wheel a little tighter and reminded herself that patience was key when dealing with a teen. Well, patience and perhaps an adults-only beach vacation. She'd have to talk to Ben and see if they could steal a few days. As the wife of a NASCAR driver, Susie knew that finding time during the NASCAR Sprint Cup Series season was going to be a challenge, but they both needed it.

"Death seems a little extreme," she said to her daughter. "I'm doing all I can to make sure everything is covered. There's only one of me. What do you expect me to do?"

"You could have picked them up before you got us from school."

Susie didn't feel compelled to explain her busy daily schedule to a fourteen-year-old. Instead, she focused on finding a parking spot by Matt's soccer field.

"Okay, buddy," she said to her son once he'd left the land of music and rejoined the family Edmonds. "I'll be back here just as soon as I've dropped Cammie at the stable. Take your water bottle and leave your music, and don't forget to—"

"I know, Mom. Have fun," Matt said before opening his door and slipping out to join his friends.

Have fun.

While her advice had been automatic, Susie found the thought a little bittersweet. When she and Ben had married, they'd decided that the one never-to-be broken rule was to find fun in everything they did. Even back in the early days, when they didn't know how they were going to scrape together the money for utility bills, let alone rent, they had always found a way to have fun. Usually it had been something as simple as a picnic lunch at their favorite park outside Mooresville.

Now they could scarcely find time for a family moment that wasn't centered on Cammie's show jumping or Matt's soccer or hockey activities. And as for couples' time? Forget it. With Ben on the road virtually every weekend during the season, and the loss of relative freedom since Susie was no longer home-schooling the children, they couldn't seem to get it in synch. She missed Ben as surely as though she hadn't seen him in months.

Cammie shifted restlessly in her seat. "Mom, if we don't leave now, how are we going to get my boots?"

"I'll pick them up tomorrow," Susie replied before pulling her cell phone from its nook in the SUV's console.

"But—"

"Sorry, sweetheart," Susie said firmly. "Right now I want to call Daddy."

"Why does it always have to be about you?" Cammie asked.

Susie had done her reading and knew the adolescent brain didn't yet fire properly, so she would cut her daughter a small amount of slack.

"Don't be rude," she said.

Cammie made the wise choice of silence.

This time, pick up the phone, Susie thought as she hit Ben's top spot on her autodial list. *Please be there.*

MID-DISCUSSION, Ben Edmonds looked down at his phone, which sat before him on the mahogany conference room table at Double S Racing. His wife's name flashed on the phone's screen, signaling her incoming call. Ben was pretty sure he'd told Susie that he'd be with his team owner and crew chief all afternoon, and probably not home for dinner, either. Pretty sure, but not positive. Life had been a little crazy lately.

"Are we distracting you from something more important, Ben?" asked Chris Sampson, who was, as far as Ben was concerned, the crew chief from hell.

"No," Ben said as he tapped his phone's Ignore feature and sent Susie off to voice mail.

"Good," the younger man flatly replied. "Now, I think we can all agree that yesterday's finish in Kansas was unacceptable."

"It goes without saying that nineteenth place is not what we're shooting for," Ben said.

"Does it?" Sampson asked.

Ben had thought he was becoming numb to the guy's barely-below-the-surface antagonism, but apparently not.

"I don't know how you got it into your head that I don't care or that I have found anything about this season acceptable," he said.

Topping the list of unacceptable events was Gil Sizemore, team owner and current silent observer at the head of the table, firing Ben's longtime crew chief and hiring Chris Sampson. Sampson was blunt to the point of rude, confrontational and nowhere near the sort of personality Ben found to be conducive to good teamwork. Beyond that, Ben was just generally ticked to have this guy shoved down his gullet.

"It's good to hear that you care because I've had my doubts," Chris replied.

Ben didn't believe in violence, but a man also had his limits. He shoved away from the table and stood, knowing he would have to walk from this room before he did something damaging. Still, he had to finish saying his piece.

"Just because I'm out of the Chase for the NASCAR Sprint Cup this season doesn't mean I don't hold myself to high standards," he said. "NASCAR was my life before you had any damn idea what a stock car might be. Sure, I don't doubt that you have your skills. Your record prior to this year has proven that. But what I can't tolerate is the lack of respect toward me. I'm putting you on notice now that the next time you make some crack about my dedication, you're going to find yourself on a whole new level of getting to know me…right down to my fist. You understand that?"

Chris rose. "I understand more than you're able to see."

"You think so?" Ben asked in a voice as distinctly unfriendly as Chris's had been.

Suddenly, though, he saw the humor in the situation. Yes, he was ticked, but he wasn't about to take on a guy probably ten years younger and definitely a whole lot meaner. Especially one who he had to find some way to work with, or a lot of people might well lose their jobs—himself included.

Gil, who had about five inches on Ben's five feet ten inches stood, too.

"Gentlemen," he said in an "I'm the boss and we'd best not be forgetting that" tone. "Why don't we all sit down and talk about what we've learned from this season? We have seven races yet to go, and I can guarantee that no progress is going to be made with you two at each other's throats."

Gil was, of course, correct…so far as his statement went. After Ben traded apologies with Chris, he took his seat but felt no better about his future. Truth was, Chris Sampson was nearly the least of Ben's issues this season. He was just the easiest to face down.

SUSIE LOVED THE NIGHTTIME. She loved the song of the crickets drifting into the bedroom through the screen door to her reading porch. And she loved the time she had alone with Ben. Or, at least Ben and the television as he sat on the sofa at the far end of their large room, watching yesterday's race with the sound muted. The only thing she didn't like was the stress that rolled off him like a storm coming in over the mountains.

"Today was a long day for you," she said as she finished off some trim on a sweater she was making for the boutique in Charlottesville. While knitting had started as a hobby—something to do with her hands because she never liked being perfectly still—it had grown into a business for her.

"I told you this morning I'd probably miss dinner,

didn't I?" Ben asked absently, gaze still fixed on the screen as he replayed a segment of race footage.

"Yes, you did. I only meant that you must be tired. I haven't seen you take a real day off in weeks," she said.

"It's the wrong time of year."

"I know, but we used to have our Mondays," she replied. Because of the NASCAR Sprint Cup schedule, Monday nights had always been their date night.

"I'd like my Mondays back, too," he replied. Still, he didn't look her way.

She wouldn't have felt so slighted except she knew that he'd be watching this same recording with his team tomorrow and had likely already looked at it earlier in the day. She wanted something of more value to her than the jewelry he'd given her over the years; she wanted his undivided attention.

Susie set aside her knitting and rose from the bed. She was aware that after sixteen years of marriage she wasn't exactly a novelty and that her long cotton night-gown was hardly alluring. Still, she also knew that Ben loved her. She crossed the room and positioned herself in front of the television.

"Babe," he said with a shake of his head. "You have to move. I can't see."

"The race will be there later."

"So will you," he replied after a brief pause.

It felt as though his words had pushed the air from her. Susie wanted to leave the bedroom…the house….

Ben stood. "I'm sorry. I didn't mean that." He rubbed his hand over his short-cut hair, making it stand even more upright than usual. "The pressure at Double S is pretty bad right now. I don't know what all I need to fix between myself, the car and the crew, but it's a lot. One hell of a lot."

The tension she'd been feeling was replaced by a different kind, but one no less difficult to hide.

"I know things haven't been good," she said. "Even if we don't talk as much as we used to, I see things, Ben. I see you. I see how frustrated you've been." She'd never been one to offer unsolicited advice, but she couldn't help herself. "Maybe you need to be a little kinder to yourself…allow yourself time to breathe."

"No. You just don't get it. I'm not a rookie. I'm not even in my prime. This is it, Susie. I'm forty-one and it's not going to get any easier."

Susie sought the right words, the right cheerful tone. "Forty-one? That's nothing, honey. Everyone says that forty is the new twenty."

He snorted. "Maybe if you're a desk jockey, but if you're a race car driver? Forty might as well be seventy in terms of reflexes. I have to be better studied and in better shape than anyone else out there. How am I going to pull that off if I don't spend more time training?"

Hello? How did she do all she did?

Even though she'd stopped homeschooling Cammie and Matt this year when they'd asked to try the local schools, between helping them keep in touch with their homeschooled friends and accommodating all the new additions to their schedules, she'd gained very little time. It seemed that work was demanding more, too. She'd hired a couple of women to do piecework for her. But Ben never asked about that part of her life, and she didn't want to burden him with more information when he was already distracted, so she kept it to herself.

"Multitask," Susie said. "It won't buy you a full day back, but it will help."

He gave her a skeptical look. "Multitask, how?"

It had sounded like a good idea in the abstract, but she struggled for an actual application.

"Well, you could put your race on the television downstairs in the exercise room and spend some time on the treadmill or even just the hot tub while you watch."

Ben's hazel eyes narrowed. "If you wanted me to watch the race in another room, all you had to do was ask."

So much for helping. Ben stalked from the room, and Susie watched the cars silently circle the track.

CHAPTER TWO

IN SIXTEEN YEARS OF MARRIAGE, Ben had never slept apart from Susie while they were under the same roof. Last night, he'd come close—too close—and it was all on him, not Susie. He was the one who'd spoken without thinking and then snarled when, in his heart, he'd known she was trying her hardest to keep peace between them. He'd joined her in bed after he'd run off some of his stress on the treadmill and then showered. She'd been sound asleep, or at least faking it. He couldn't blame her if she had. He'd barely been able to tolerate himself. And early this morning, she'd already been downstairs having breakfast with Cammie and Matt when he'd risen, so they'd had no chance to talk.

Now, as he drove past the stone pillars marking the entry to Havenhurst Country Club, Ben didn't feel a whole lot better. Even though he was a couple of minutes overdue for a breakfast meeting with his agent, he bypassed the valet parking and pulled into the lot. Once parked, he reached for his cell phone and debated calling Susie. She'd be on the road, he knew. Doing what, he didn't.

Though Ben hadn't argued the point too strenuously, he hadn't wanted her to stop home-schooling the kids. That had always given them the flexibility to be on the road with him. Since late August, he'd been traveling without them. Although he remained surrounded by the dozens of people involved in keeping a NASCAR team up and running, the nights alone were tough.

Ben was just getting ready to call Susie when his screen flashed with the notice of an incoming text message. He smiled when he saw it was from his wife; she detested texting and said she'd do it only with those she really, *really* loved. Despite his stupid behavior last night, he must still be on that list. Ben opened the message.

Am meeting with friends at 8:30 tonight. Please be home to watch C and M. Thanks.

Usually her texts ended with ILY—short for I love you. Thanks fell far short of that.

"My fault," he reminded himself.

He'd make up for last night. Ripples in his professional life shouldn't affect her or the kids. Ben closed Susie's text and exited the car. He was looking forward to his meeting with Kane Ledger. The guy was a straight shooter and a good source for business advice, too. Ben needed him for both attributes this morning.

As Ben made his way through the club's nearly imposing front door and to the dining room, he returned greetings from the many friends he'd made in his years belonging here. It blew his mind to think that a Tennessee farm boy had grown up to become a NASCAR driver and golf lover, but here he was.

The maître d' showed Ben to a windowside table where Kane already waited. Ben's agent stood and shook his hand. Ben believed in vibes and instinct, and both were already telling him that this would not be an upbeat meeting. He'd let Kane take the lead, though. No sense in inviting trouble when it seemed to be appearing at his doorstep daily already.

After ordering eggs, bacon and wheat toast, and getting a little caffeine into his system by way of coffee, Ben eased into conversation with Kane. They had moved on to shop talk about the weekend's upcoming race in California when the food arrived. Ben was two bites into his eggs when Kane spoke.

"I've got some news for you, and it's not good," he said. "Hometeam Insurance has been in contact with Gil Sizemore and me. At this point, they won't be renewing their sponsorship for next season."

Appetite gone, Ben pushed aside his plate.

This wasn't just a small sponsorship with a sticker on the car's B-post; this was Ben's primary sponsorship. His car had been painted the Hometeam colors of navy blue with red and gold accents, and covered with its logos for almost a decade. The company had paid millions of dollars annually for the privilege, too. Teams folded and drivers lost rides over a departing main sponsor. In this case, Gil Sizemore would be fine. He had other drivers, with other sponsors. Ben stood at much greater risk.

"Did they say why?" he asked.

Kane hesitated before speaking, something Ben had seldom seen him do.

"I think it's a number of things. Money is tighter in the insurance business, and everyone is looking for ways to reduce expenses."

"So we'll just cut a new deal with them. I can do more promo work and attend more corporate events, too."

"I've already offered that," Kane replied. "It was a no go."

The problem with a straight shooter as an agent was taking those blows straight to the gut.

A nod was pretty much all Ben could work up in response. He followed that with a coffee chaser to see if he could lose some of the numbness that seemed to be working its way from the inside out.

"This is rough, but it could be worse," Kane said. "There won't be a public announcement by Hometeam unless they settle on someone else to sponsor, and I'm going to do all I can to keep the lines of communication open. The real issue is a loss of confidence that you're going to get them the exposure they want for that kind of money."

Ben couldn't help but defend himself.

"Exposure comes in a lot of forms. Even if my finishes have been down the past couple of years, my website still has one of the most active forums out there. I get more discussion and more hits than just about anyone but Kent Grosso, and Hometeam's color and logos are all over the site."

"I agree your fans are active, but I'm also beginning to read some unhappiness," Kane replied after a bite of his breakfast. "They're losing faith in your ability on the track. They still respect the way you mentor other drivers and they applaud your volunteer work. But even then, I've seen some concern that your activities are affecting your driving, too."

"You're sure sifting a lot from a pack of one-sentence posts," Ben said.

"It's my job to know what's going on with you," Kane

replied. "And I do…at least on the surface. Do you have anything else you think I need to know?"

Ben didn't want to talk about any of this. If Kane had been keeping an eye on the fan forum, he had also seen the idle chat about when Ben might be retiring. The whole damn topic had him rattled.

"No," he said to his agent. "At least not now, with this Hometeam thing to absorb. I've got a lot of thinking to do."

"Okay," Kane said. "And in the meantime, I've already talked to the team about putting out quiet feelers to your secondary sponsors to see if anyone is interested in a bigger investment. We've had some curiosity. If you stay in at least the top quarter of finishers for the rest of the season, we might get something going."

Time was, Ben might have felt hungry and ready to grab at success when faced with a challenge like that. Now the prospect of cold scrambled eggs seemed more attractive. Ben returned to his breakfast knowing it was going to be a helluva long day.

WHEN SHE COULD WRANGLE the time, Susie always loved going to Maudie's Down Home Diner to meet with the group of women who affectionately referred to themselves as the Tuesday Tarts. Tonight, she almost hadn't made it. Even though Ben had sent her a text saying he'd be home to watch the kids, he hadn't shown up. At first, she'd resigned herself to staying home. Cammie had pointed out, though, that if she was old enough to babysit for other families, she could watch Matt for a few hours. And so Susie had come to the one location where all those connected to NASCAR could relax and be themselves. Yet tonight she felt restless, sad and strangely out of place.

It wasn't the company. Sheila Trueblood, the diner's owner, was her same hospitable, sharp and funny self. The women present were also as they had always been…laughing and talking about everything from last weekend's race in Kansas to their favorite authors. Right now, Susie's dear friend Patsy Grosso, co-owner of Cargill-Grosso Racing, was listing off-site places to visit if anyone had a few spare minutes at this weekend's upcoming race outside of Los Angeles. Happiness fairly glowed in the small yet comfortable seating area that occupied part of the diner's storage room.

Because it would be rude to just walk out, Susie checked her cell phone and gave a shake of her head, as though she'd just received a text message that was a bit of a bother. Then she did as she'd been yearning and rose to step out of the confines of the back room.

"Is everything okay, Susie?" asked Patsy.

Susie worked up a smile. "Fine…I just need to call home. Cammie has a question for me."

Patsy laughed. "It's funny how critical it is for our families to hunt us down during our 'me' time, isn't it?"

"We become indispensable the moment we step away," said fellow Tart Cara Stallworth, a mother of three.

Keeping her expression bright, Susie waggled her phone in her hand and said, "Let me take care of this, and I'll be right back in."

Susie slipped from the back room and into the diner, which had only a few customers at this time of the night. She was thankful for both the relative quiet and the fact that she needn't keep that cheerful expression pinned on when she was away from her friends. Her face was beginning to ache.

Susie settled into a booth far from the other customers, closed her eyes, tipped back her head and let calm wash over her. She felt a little guilty for scamming her friends in the other room, but not enough so that she was about to go back in there. She needed this moment to collect herself. She had relaxed just about to the tips of her toes when a sound from behind her jolted her back to full awareness. She swung around so that she was able to peer over the back of the booth.

Mellie Donovan, Maudie's waitress and occasional Tuesday Tart, had just set down refilled salt and pepper shakers at the table. It was no great commotion, but it didn't take much to rattle Susie these days.

"Mellie, you nearly scared me to death!" she said, lightening the drama of her words with a shaky laugh.

"I'm sorry," the younger woman replied quietly. "Everybody's served and happy, so I'm trying to get some side work done while I can. It seems like I don't have enough hours in the day."

Susie could relate. "Isn't that the truth? I feel as though lately I've had a chain of endlessly long days."

Mellie hefted a second set of salt and pepper shakers that she still held in her left hand. "I keep looking for the upside to schedules like ours. The best I've come up with is that I'd rather be wildly busy than bored."

Susie could scarcely recall Mellie ever standing still— or talking this much. With her short-cropped black hair and delicate features, she hardly looked old enough to hold a job let alone have a three-year-old daughter, yet Susie knew she did. Mellie and her daughter, Lily, lived in an apartment above the diner. And because Maudie's was truly a big family, Louise Jordan, wife to cook Al, was Lily's daycare provider while Mellie worked. But based by the baby monitor that Mellie carried, tonight Lily must have been sound asleep upstairs.

"Somehow, I doubt you're ever bored," Susie said.

"I have no time for bored, though someday I'd like to try it out," the waitress replied.

Susie hesitated before asking, "Would it be okay if you sat with me for a couple of minutes?"

She liked the quiet younger woman and felt right now as though they were kindred spirits. Susie was as emotionally restless as Mellie was tense.

The waitress looked around the diner, then without so much as a nod, sat.

Faint purplish shadows showed beneath Mellie's brown eyes, and Susie felt a stab of remorse for complaining about long days when this girl worked them just to survive.

"I know it's none of my business, but you seem kind of sad. If you'd like someone to talk to…" Mellie trailed off, then shook her head. "I'm sorry. That sounded silly. You've got a roomful of friends back there."

Susie did, indeed. But those friends were all intimately connected with NASCAR, whether as a team owner, team employee or wife of a driver. All of them had known Ben for years. Susie could never get past a feeling of disloyalty if she were to tell them how worried she was about her husband, both because of his self-confidence issues on the track and because of the disconnect that had popped up in their marriage. She didn't feel comfortable giving Mellie the particulars, either, but she could talk in generalities.

"Have you ever felt as though things are spinning out of control?" she asked Mellie.

The girl nodded. "Lily just turned three. Things are always spinning out of control."

"Good point. It's been a while for me, but I remember those days."

Susie tilted her head as she recalled how much busier, yet simpler, life had been for her family even seven years ago, when Matt had been three. Ben had been doing well and was fairly consistently in the Chase. She'd been totally in love with homeschooling Cammie and Matt, and their course in life had seemed so clear. Not so much, these days.

"So, does it get less busy as children get older?" Mellie asked, breaking into Susie's reverie.

"It's busy, but a different kind of busy. You don't have to worry so much about those toddler-proofing issues, but that gained time is taken up by being sure they're doing what they should at school and by getting them where they need to be. It's just as tough keeping up, but exciting to see them grow and change."

"The changes I see in Lily just over a week or so are amazing," the younger woman said. "She learns new words almost every day and gets a little bolder about trying to boss me around, too."

Thinking of Cammie, Susie laughed. "Trust me, that won't change."

"My life is a lot to handle between work and Lily, but I'll do whatever it takes to keep her safe and loved," she said with a fierceness that Susie had never before heard from her. She was sure there was something else going on, but Mellie didn't continue.

And after listening to the younger woman's determination in the face of such challenges, Susie knew that it was time to stop fretting and start doing when it came to her family. After all, family was everything.

One of the customers began to stir, and Mellie rose.

"I'd better get moving," she said.

"Of course," Susie replied, then smiled. "And Mellie?"

"Yes?"

"Thank you."

An expression of surprise passed over the young woman's face. "For what?"

"A long overdue reminder," Susie replied, then rose, too.

Mellie shook her head. "I don't know what I did, but you're welcome."

And Susie would not forget.

Back in the Tarts' corner of the world, conversation rolled on, fueled by coffee and some sinfully rich brownies that Sheila had baked.

"Is everything okay at home?" Sheila asked when Susie reentered the room. "You were out there for a while."

"Everything's fine," Susie assured her.

Or at least it would be fine after she brought back some of the "good old days" into her family in hopes that Ben's optimism, which he'd had so much of back then, would also return. Once he was back to normal, Susie would relax, and the kids would benefit from both of those changes.

Susie settled next to Patsy on a plump love seat. Patsy smiled at her in acknowledgment, and Susie smiled back. She had looked up to Patsy, who was a bit older, forever.

Patsy Grosso was one of those women who managed to look put together in nothing more exotic than a pair of jeans and a crisp white shirt. Susie was more the bohemian skirt and a colorful hand-knit sweater sort, but over the years she'd grown comfortable with who she was.

"So, tell me again what you're thinking of doing in California this weekend?" she asked her friend in a low voice as other conversations swirled and eddied around them.

"Does this mean you're actually coming to the race?" Patsy asked in response.

"I think so. I'd like to surprise Ben by showing up there with the kids. I'm also hoping I can talk him into playing hooky for a day or so after the race, too."

"That sounds wonderful! Though I understand why you had to let Cammie have some say in her high school years, I know Ben misses having all of you around," Patsy said.

Susie nodded. "I'm not sure I'll be able to pull this off. I need to check commercial flights. Since Ben can't know what I'm up to, we can hardly tag along on his charter flight."

"We have room on our plane. Just come with us on Saturday morning and then book a commercial flight back."

"Are you sure?"

"Absolutely. We have plenty of room this weekend, and Dean and I haven't had time with Cammie and Matt in ages. Let me know if there's anything else I can do to help."

"You're doing enough already. Thank you so much," Susie said.

This was going to work! By the time they came back from California, her family would be back in kilter.

CHAPTER THREE

A SATURDAY AFTERNOON in sunny Southern California was far from a bad thing. Ben relaxed on a lounge chair outside his motor home and used his laptop computer to respond to a couple of questions on his fan site. After he finished catching up, he planned to do something really decadent such as read a book and doze in the sunshine. He smiled at the thought. There was a time when he'd want to be out kicking up a little fun instead of kicking back. Today, this suited him just fine.

Ben had just shut his laptop and his eyes when he heard the scuff of footsteps coming his way. Without even looking, he knew it was Darrell, his motor home driver/cook. Darrell's lazy gait had grown heavier over the years, as had Darrell. No surprise, though. His cooking made Ben the envy of all the other drivers, and Ben a big fan of working out.

"Hey, hate to mess up your afternoon, but Chris needs you at the garage right now. He says it's important," Darrell announced.

That was enough to make Ben open his eyes. "And he sent you?"

The larger man shrugged. "I was over that way, so I guess he decided I was easier than a phone call."

It wasn't a matter of ease. Sampson flat-out liked ordering people around, and Ben was tempted to ignore the demand even if it had been couched in terms of a request. He'd already told his crew chief that his goal was a quiet afternoon, but what he'd really been shooting for was a Sampson-free one. Ben had qualified a very respectable twelfth, practiced well earlier this morning, and for once the crew wasn't tense. Since he didn't want to see those dynamics change before the race tomorrow, he gave up on his idea of paradise.

"All right," he said, rising from the lounge. "So much for a semilazy Saturday. Would you mind sticking my computer back inside?"

"No problem," Darrell replied.

As Ben covered the relatively short distance from the drivers' and owners' lot to the garages, he readied himself to keep his calm in the face of his crew chief's abrasive bluntness. Leading by example was a belief that anchored Ben's world. He would not let Sampson change that.

The area directly around Ben's garage stall was pretty much a ghost town, but that wasn't unusual since a NASCAR Nationwide Series race was about to start out on the track. Most everyone would have their attention turned in that direction.

Ben shielded his eyes from the sunshine as he looked into the dimmer garage.

"Chris? You in there?"

No one answered so he stepped inside.

"Hello?"

Still no one. He was about to turn away from this fool's mission when Susie, Matt and Cammie popped up from behind the No. 515 car.

"Surprise!" they cried in unison.

Ben laughed.

"You've got to be kidding me," he said, holding his arms out to his family. "Darrell set me up, didn't he? How did you get here?"

Agile Matt was first in for a hug. The boy was destined to be an athlete of some sort.

"Uncle Dean and Aunt Patsy were coming in early this morning and they let us ride on their jet!"

"That's great," Ben said, ruffling the top of his son's short-cut hair. Matt insisted on having the same cut as Ben, which Ben found both flattering and funny. Except for Matt's eyes, which were identical to Susie's, the kid was pretty much his Mini-Me.

Susie was next in line for a hug. He drew his wife close and said, "I've missed you" before he kissed her.

How he loved this woman—not just because of the way she felt so right in his arms or because she'd given him two wonderful children, either. He loved that she would do this for him when he'd been nothing short of a rabid bear around the house lately.

Without leaving the circle of his arms, Susie went up on tiptoe.

"You have no idea how much I've missed you," she murmured before stepping back.

Ben tucked away that sweet thought and focused on Cammie.

"Do you have a hug for me?"

"Sure," she said, then meandered forward with no apparent enthusiasm.

Ben had known that his daughter was going to hit those adolescent too-cool-to-have-parents years. Heck, every kid did; he didn't take it personally. And he knew that Susie was handling Cammie with the same big heart and steel backbone that she had to use with him. And because he had Susie to back him up, Ben could afford to be a little goofy with his girl.

"Time for a Cammie whammy," he said, then picked her up and spun her in a crazy circle, just as he had since she'd been little.

"Dad!" she protested, but Ben heard the laughter she fought to hold in.

When he set her back on her sneaker-shod feet, she gave him her dimpled smile, one that had always melted his heart.

"You're so weird," she said.

"Yup, and you'd better get used to it, kiddo."

Ben turned his attention to Susie. "It just so happens that I scheduled the afternoon off. Let me have Darrell round up a car, and we'll all get away from here for a while, okay?"

"Sounds like heaven," she replied.

Ben smiled. He was ready to kick up some fun once again.

"HOME, SWEET HOME," Susie said to Ben as they walked toward the motor home after a dinner with one of Ben's sponsors.

She was glad that she'd left a small wardrobe in the motor home even after knowing she wouldn't be traveling this season. A dress and a pair of pumps hadn't quite made her packing list last night. She'd been more about race wear and beach wear.

"We've had this place longer than we have our real home," Ben said as he held open the door for her.

"And it cost far more than our first house, so no wonder we've held on to it," Susie said as she climbed the three steps into the comfortable interior.

Once inside, she slipped off her shoes, picked them up and tucked them into what Matt had always called the shoe jail. She'd had her rules about keeping the interior. It might be spacious for one, but even as big as it was, it could be snug for a family of four. And family had been the thought when she and Ben had worked on modifying the interior design.

In addition to the master bedroom, Matt and Cammie each had a bunk bed with lots of closet space nearby. The kitchen was as well equipped as Susie's at home, if not as large. She'd also had cupboards fitted to hold the children's school supplies since learning hadn't stopped just because they'd been on the road. Susie had made it an adventure, writing her lesson plans around their location. The oak dining table and chairs had seen many a classroom session as well as family dinner.

Truly, Susie missed this place even though she knew they'd made the best decision for Cammie, and eventually Matt, by staying home. High school was about learning social skills as well as book skills. They couldn't be on the road half of the school year and do the experience justice.

Ben had tucked away his shoes and was taking his usual spot on the tan leather sofa. Even before he'd settled in, he was wrenching off his tie and unbuttoning the top button of his dress shirt. Susie smiled at the familiar sight. Ben had never been a "fancy dress" man. For all that had changed, thank heaven some things hadn't.

"Thanks for coming along tonight," he said.

"You're welcome. It actually felt nice to get dressed up and meet new people. I just hope it's going as well on Dean and Patsy's end."

"I'm sure they're doing fine," Ben said, his voice

rough with tiredness…or maybe a little desire. Susie couldn't be sure.

The Grossos had insisted on taking Cammie and Matt overnight. They had brought them along to a special evening party at a big amusement park. Susie hoped all the activity was going to keep Cammie's mind off the fact that she'd had to withdraw from today's horse show. The girl was every bit as competitive as her father, and Susie knew this hadn't sat well.

Sleepy and a little jet-lagged, Susie curled up in her favorite place in the world—against Ben's chest. The sure and steady beat of his heart was a comfort that could never be equaled.

"It sounds as though qualifying went well," she said.

"The best in a long time. And the crew seems to have it together…no friction at all. I think we've got a shot at a win, and I'd almost forgotten what that feels like," he replied as he smoothed a hand down the bare skin of her arm.

"I'm even happier we're here, then."

"Me, too." He hesitated before saying, "Honey, I know I owe you an apology. I haven't been much fun to be around and I'm really sorry for that."

Susie sat upright so that she could see his face. He was so solemn that her heart ached for him…for them.

"We're going through some adjustments, that's all," she said. "It will all be fine."

He ran a hand through his hair, a gesture of distraction that Susie had seen much too frequently as of late.

"Probably," he said.

She gave him the best sexy and teasing look she could

summon. "*Probably?* Probably doesn't take the bull by the horns. And probably doesn't win races, either, mister."

Ben laughed. "Someone's feeling a little sassy tonight."

Susie stood, then moved so that she could brace her hands on the couch's back either side of her husband. She leaned in and gave him a quick, passionate kiss…a promise of more intimacy to come.

"I want you to note carefully that I am not going to say the word probably," she said. "Because probably won't get you what's going to be waiting on the other side of that bedroom door, either."

Just then, the motor home's door swung open. Susie's back was to the door, but Ben had a clear view of their visitor.

"Cammie, is everything all right?" he asked as Suzie turned to face her daughter.

Cammie was already clad in her favorite pink flannel sleep pants and T-shirt. In contrast to that happy hue, her expression was the closed-off one Susie had been seeing more frequently…both from her daughter and her husband.

"No, everything's not all right. My stomach hurts after the rides and the stuff I ate," Cammie announced. "I couldn't sleep, so I told Aunt Patsy I was walking back here."

"By yourself?" Susie asked automatically while she fully returned from thoughts of lovemaking to parenthood.

Cammie rolled her eyes. "Mom, they're like five spots away from here, and the lot has security."

"Is Matt staying there?" Ben asked.

"Yes," Cammie replied. "He and Uncle Dean are playing video games. Can I go to bed now? I don't want to talk." With that, she walked to her bunk, climbed in and curled into a fetal position facing the motor home's outer skin.

Susie looked down at Ben, who gave her a crooked smile.

"We might as well turn in, too," he said.

"Leave the bathroom light on," Cammie said. "Just in case I need to barf."

"Okay, honey," Susie replied.

Romance.

Susie remembered the concept in a vague sort of way....

BEN WOKE SLOWLY as the sun drifted through blinds that had been turned to let morning approach lazily. The rattle and clink of dishware and the deadly delicious smell of bacon frying came to him from the main living area. He couldn't believe that good-nutrition Susie would be frying up his favorite kind of breakfast, but it seemed that she was since she'd also told Darrell to take a breather for the rest of the weekend. Ben pulled on a robe and exited the bedroom.

Already showered and dressed for the day, his wife stood in front of the stove. Cammie's bunk was empty, but she was nowhere in sight.

"Where's Little Miss Sunshine?" Ben asked Susie, who smiled over at him. Cammie was not, and never had been, a morning person.

"She headed back over to Dean and Patsy's to pick up her overnight bag and apparently seek a breakfast not involving fried animal flesh...her words, not mine."

"So she's a vegetarian now?"

Susie shrugged. "This morning, at least. But you, my love, remain a carnivore, and that's who I cooked for."

He went to stand behind his wife, wrapped his arms around her and planted a kiss on his favorite sweet spot, just below her right ear.

"Thank you," he said.

She smiled back over her shoulder at him. "Have a seat. I'm almost finished up here."

It was apparent she'd been busy for some time, too. The table had been set with shiny silver and real cloth napkins. What looked to be fresh squeezed orange juice awaited them in a glass pitcher with three fancy glasses he hadn't even known were in the galley. No surprise, since Darrell wasn't much for presentation.

"At least let me take my plate to the table," he offered.

"It's race day," she replied. "And the first one in months I've been here to pamper you, so let me do it."

Ben smiled. "I guess I won't argue with that."

"Good choice," she replied as she loaded a crockery bowl with scrambled eggs. Susie had always cooked as though feeding an army, and he'd been happy to make up the difference for the thin ranks.

Ben sat and watched his wife bring the eggs in one hand and a plate of bacon in the other.

"I'll be back with the toast in just a second," she said.

Damn, but he liked the way she looked in the morning.

"Take your time," he said. "I'm enjoying the view."

She gave him an amused look and was about to take the toast from the toaster when Carrie Underwood's voice began to ring out from someplace Ben couldn't fathom.

"My cell phone, bless it all," Susie said, then pulled a hot pink little number from her knitting bag on the sofa. "I upgraded to add internet service on Friday and I swear my volume of mail and calls increased just to prove I wasn't being extravagant." She looked at the phone's screen. "Do you mind if I take this? It's business."

How could he mind after all she'd done? And as for the extravagance of a new cell phone, Ben figured he was already bleeding money from a thousand paper cuts. One more financial nick was pretty negligible.

While Susie headed into the bathroom to take the call, he finished up the toast and brought it to the table. And by the time she returned, his stomach had moved on from a growl straight to a roar.

"I'm sorry about the delay," she said as she took her spot opposite him. "You should have started without me," she added once she'd noted his sparkling clean white plate.

"That wouldn't have been very gentlemanly of me," he replied, then served himself a mountain of fluffy eggs.

"Thank you," she said.

"Interesting choice of location for a phone call," he said as he poured her some juice.

"I'm sorry. I didn't want to distract you with my little bit of nonsense when you have to stay focused today."

Ben smiled. "Not *that* focused. You said it was business?"

Susie nodded. "That was the owner of a chain of boutiques back home. We've been playing phone tag for a week, so I wanted to catch her while I could."

"A chain of boutiques?" Ben gave a low whistle. "Are you going to have time to keep up with all that knitting?"

She busied herself spooning out a minuscule portion of eggs and replied, "I'll work it out."

Ben knew that at some point or another her knitting had become more than a hobby. How much more, he wasn't sure. Susie handled the household accounts and their business manager, in conjunction with Ben, everything else. Whatever she spent or brought in on knitting supplies fell within Susie's domain.

"Well, if you need a sounding board, you know I'm here, right?" he asked.

Susie nodded. "I know, but there's no reason to draw you in. It's nothing, really, when compared to everything you do. It's just enough to give me a little fun money."

Ben was about to tell her that it didn't have to be about the money, except in his life, it did. The money and the points. He took a deep swallow of juice to fight back the tension working its way into his bones. Damn, but sometimes he wished he could knit.

CHAPTER FOUR

SUSIE LOOKED AT HER REFLECTION in the full-length mirror on the back of the bathroom door. She made it a habit to dress in Ben's colors on race day, and today's choice of navy linen pants and a gold top with a red-and-gold silk scarf at the neckline fit the bill. More classy than flashy.

"Not bad for sitting square on forty years old," she murmured, smoothing the pants over her hips.

Despite the detour last night had taken, Susie was ready to head straight on into the day. The first order of business would be to share with Ben the plans she'd made for a two-day minivacation about one hundred miles south of the track, on Coronado Island. She'd found the most marvelous old hotel, replete with charm, a beautiful beach and even a ghost for Cammie, who was into that ghost/vampire/impossible romance thing.

After one last check of her makeup, she left the bathroom and joined her family in the main living area. It was tradition that they walked to the pit area together before the start of each race.

"Are we ready?" she asked.

"I'd be readier if I could have been in the horse show yesterday," Cammie said from the sofa where she sat with her cell phone between her hands. Susie sometimes wondered if it was going to become permanently affixed to her daughter.

Matt, who was wearing a smaller version of Ben's team shirt, wrinkled his nose at his sister. "Huh? That doesn't even make sense. If you were in the horse show, then—"

"Who cares what you think?" Cammie grumped. "Andrea Holton won both the junior hunter and the equitation championships, and I know I could have beaten her."

"Not from California," Matt smugly replied.

"Well, duh!"

"You just miss Symphony. You're in *loooove* with your horsey," Matt teased, then made a series of wet kissing noises that had Cammie looking like a thundercloud.

"Enough," Susie said in a firm voice. "We need to get out to the track."

"Before World War Three erupts," Ben muttered under his breath.

They left the motor home not so much the crew Ben used to say they were, but more a small, warring nation.

"It's not fair," Cammie said as she trailed three steps behind the rest of the family on their way to the pits. "I shouldn't have had to miss that show. You could have left me with one of the other families from the barn, or left me home alone. I'm responsible enough."

Matt snickered. "Want me to tell Mom and Dad how you locked us out of the house last week, and I had to climb in the window?"

"Thanks," Cammie snapped. "You just did."

"You're welcome," Matt replied. "Your horse is way smarter than you are and nobody lets him stay alone."

"You are *such* a miserable brat! I don't want to travel with you ever again."

Susie had been trying to be patient, but no reward seemed to be coming from it. Ignoring the people milling around them, she stopped dead in her tracks so that Cammie had to swerve to avoid her. When her daughter was within reach, Susie settled a hand on her arm.

"I'm going to say this once," she said quietly. "Life is not always all about you. We are a family, and on this one weekend…this one day…it's about your father. He's given you every opportunity and every bit of support you could ever desire. Without him, there would be no Symphony to ride or custom boots to wear while riding. Dad deserves our support right now. He needs us. Can you understand that?"

Cammie nodded. "Sorry. I'll stop."

She gave her daughter's arm a comforting squeeze. "Good girl."

She had never said anything directly to the children about their dad's racing season, but she was well aware that others had been less sensitive.

"Now put on a smile, okay?"

Cammie's smile reminded Susie of the forced baring of teeth she'd produced when she'd first had her picture taken with Santa. That was good enough for Susie, though. She quickened her pace to join Ben, but once she'd matched her stride to his, she wished she hadn't. His jaw was set as though his back molars had locked together, and his narrowed gaze shot straight forward.

"Sunny and cool. It's a great day for a race," she said.

Ben nodded, but said nothing. He tended to be intense before a race, but seldom to the point of coolness toward her.

Then it occurred to Susie: *He'd heard.*

As quiet as she'd tried to be, he'd heard her talking about his need for support. Ben was a born leader, and as one, he always gave and expected nothing in return. Had she somehow made him feel diminished with her words? Susie could hardly fathom it, but she could also hardly fathom many other recent changes in her husband. All she wanted to do was make things better, but until she fully understood Ben's issues, how could she expect to do that?

Talk to me, please, she thought. But this was what her marriage was becoming—a silent plea falling on deaf ears. Both she and Ben were to blame, really. And though she could do nothing about Ben, she could fix herself. Susie squared her shoulders and bolstered her grit. The time for subtleties had passed.

BEN CLIMBED OUT of the No. 515 car, pulled off his helmet and took the bottle of water offered to him by a crew member. Even though he wasn't much of a drinker, he knew he'd be wishing for something stronger by the time Sampson had finished with him.

Two hundred laps…four hundred miles…and Ben was right back to where he'd started—nowhere at all. Between damage from a piece of debris that had required a longer pit stop than usual, another just generally bad pit, and a couple of missed opportunities on his part, even though he'd started twelfth, he had finished twenty-third. The only good news was that fellow Double S driver Rafael O'Bryan took first, so for now, at least, Gil Sizemore would be occupied by more pleasant things than giving Ben the list of his failings during this race.

While heading into his hauler's war room for the race postmortem, Ben kept his head down and avoided those few people from the media who even tried to approach him. If he couldn't deliver at least an uplifting message, he preferred to keep his mouth shut. And today he felt slogged down in a sea of bull. Uplifting was out of the question.

"What's your first impression?" Ben's crew chief asked before Ben had even closed the door to the cool and quiet wood-paneled war room. Neither had he even looked up from the clipboard in front of him.

Chris Sampson, unlike the Sampson of yore, did not have long, flowing locks, but close-clipped blond hair. Had it been otherwise, Ben would have found some way to shave his crew chief's head and get rid of a measure of the man's power.

"Mistakes were made," Ben replied after he settled into a leather club chair a few down from where the crew chief was seated. "On my end and in other places."

"Let's start with your end."

"Okay. It's pretty clear that I could have blocked Kent Grosso and blew it. I also let Bart Branch push me up on the wall. My fault on both counts and I'm not denying it."

"Good. Neither am I."

For the first time in his racing career, Ben didn't feel at least an equal to his crew chief. With Steve, his former crew chief, life had been markedly different. Respect had flourished, and Steve had always been willing to admit when he'd screwed up. The same wasn't true with Chris. Not once this season had Sampson admitted to a tactical error during a race. And while the guy was undeniably good, he was also human.

"How about you?" Ben asked. "What do you see from your end that could be tightened?"

"I'll address that with the rest of the team. I'm focusing on you at this moment. And my question is pretty simple—where is your head?"

Ben could think of numerous rude responses, but didn't voice any of them.

"Exactly where it should be," he replied.

"Is it? Because I've got the feeling you're not into the game anymore." Sampson finally set aside the clipboard, placing it on a low table to his right. "It's okay, you know. Not many drivers stay in the game as long as you have or achieve even a quarter of what you have, too. It's okay to get tired and want to move on."

Ben tried to absorb what the man was saying. Was this about no longer being part of the Double S team, or was it something even more unthinkable?

"Are you talking about retirement?" he asked.

"Well…yeah. Are you going to tell me that the thought has never entered your mind?"

"Not in a good way, it hasn't."

Thumbing through a magazine on the way out to California, Ben had read about a Japanese corporate business practice that had once existed. Executives a company no longer found useful were not forced out; they were simply put in a windowless room with others of their sort and no work to do. Ben knew there was no such office at Double S's headquarters, but he knew right down to the marrow of his bones how those execs had felt—empty.

"Retirement is neither good nor bad," the crew chief

said. "It just *is*. One day, we all retire. It's something we need to accept."

A pretty Zen-like notion, and easier to produce for a man in his thirties who likely had thirty more years in front of him in his chosen career. Ben knew he was looking at a handful of years at most.

"The good news is I don't need your permission or encouragement to retire. That's mine to choose to consider when and as I please," he told Sampson. "But let me tell you what I do need. I do need you to be a crew chief, with all the job entails. Let's flip the mirror and ask you how you feel about your performance. Do you feel you've been a team builder? Are you happy with the condition of the car? Do you think you've had a positive impact on us this season?"

Ben stopped there, knowing that frustration and a measure of something damn dark like dread gripped him.

The younger man frowned. "That's not what we're here to discuss."

"No, that's not what *you're* here to discuss. I raised it because we're equals, and I'm allowed to ask you those kinds of questions if you're allowed to grill me on retirement plans, don't you think?"

"I didn't grill you."

Ben grinned though he wasn't feeling especially happy. "Then explain the burn marks you keep leaving on my ass."

If Sampson had an answer to that, he didn't stick around to hear it.

Retirement? Ben never wanted to hear that word again.

SUSIE STOOD in front of the motor home's open refrigerator and peered inside as though the answer to her husband's problems might be lurking behind the milk. It wasn't, though the milk would come in handy with Cammie and Matt, who were outside toasting marshmallows over the barbecue grill. Functioning on autopilot, she pulled the milk, set it on the counter, then found two plastic tumblers.

It had been a miserable race for Ben, and she was running short of ways to make him see that this was just a slump and not a death knell sounding. Earlier in the season, she'd gone as far as making a chart so that Ben could see in graphic color the number of times a mechanical failure, an accident caused by someone else or just plain old bad luck had hindered him. Ben had feigned interest, but she'd known it was just that—a game of Let's Humor Susie.

All she had left to pull out of her bag of tricks was some enforced relaxation. If she couldn't help him get his head on straight, maybe with some time away from Double S, he'd do it for himself.

Susie took the milk in one hand, the tumblers in the other and walked out the open door.

"You can't have s'mores without milk," she said to her children. "That would be just flat out wrong."

Cammie, who had finally managed to let go of the horse show drama, played along saying, "Like almost un-American."

Susie set the milk and glasses next to the graham crackers and chocolate bars on the outdoor dining table that always traveled with them.

"You want me to make you one, Mom?" Matt asked.

Her taste buds would love it, but the fit of her clothes, not so much.

"Thanks for the offer, but not right now, sweetie," she said.

Ben would be back soon. She wanted to have his usual postrace iced tea ready, along with a fluffy towel near the shower. The first several years he'd driven, he'd been too keyed up to sleep or even sit still the night after a race. Now he wanted a cool drink, a hot shower, a nap and a meal—in that precise order.

Just then she saw Ben approaching. Until the instant he'd noticed her watching, his expression had been grim. The effort he'd taken to look relaxed was something she could feel all these yards away.

"Want a s'more, Dad?" Matt asked when he was near enough.

"No thanks, buddy," Ben replied. "It's time for me to go in and shower up."

"Okay," Matt said, then turned his attention back to his marshmallow.

Susie followed Ben inside, then closed the door as a hint to Cammie and Matt that the adults needed a little chat time.

"It's been one hell of a day," Ben said.

Since just about all Susie could think to say in the way of encouragement was, "Well, at least twenty-third is nearly middle of the pack," she chose to keep quiet.

In an echo of her earlier behavior, he opened the refrigerator door and stared silently inside. After several seconds of apparent deliberation, he came out with a beer.

"Really?" Susie asked, both because it was beer and because she had his tea waiting on the dining table.

"Absolutely," he replied as he twisted off the bottle cap and set it on the counter. "It's been that bad."

"It must be. I can't say I've ever seen you pass over sweet tea for beer immediately after a race."

"It's not the race. It's dealing with Sampson," Ben replied, then took a long swallow, after which he added, "Though the race was no big prize, either."

"Except for those two slow pit stops, it looked pretty good," she fibbed.

Ben gave her a skeptical look. "You've been at this long enough to know where I screwed up."

"Yes, and I agree there was a lost opportunity and a little loose driving, but the pit stops are where you really lost the time."

"Better. We've been together for too long for you to humor me."

Susie laughed as she picked up the beer cap and deposited it in the below-counter trash can. "You think?"

His smile was slow in coming, but very real once it arrived. "Okay, bad choice of words. Humor me at will."

"Actually, I've been thinking more in terms of having you humor me."

He walked to the sofa and sat down. "That sounds interesting. How?"

"I've reserved us rooms at the most fabulous hotel on Coronado Island," Susie said as she seated herself next to Ben. "It's old and kind of fancy-looking, yet laid-back at the same time. Matt and Cammie can explore, and you and I can have some quiet time, and maybe talk a little?"

"So you have this set up for right after the season ends? That sounds great."

"Actually, the reservations are a little earlier than that."

"How much earlier?"

"Like tomorrow."

He sighed. "Honey, you know I can't just take off during the season."

"It wouldn't be that long. I have a rental car being delivered here in the morning, and reservations for all of us to fly out of San Diego early Wednesday morning. Since next weekend's race is right there in Charlotte, this will barely take a nip out of your schedule. An extra forty-eight hours away from the garage won't be the end of civilization as we know it."

"It depends when those forty-eight hours occur, and this isn't a good time. How much did the hotel cost?" Ben asked.

"Somewhat less than a fortune," Susie replied.

She wanted to tell him that she'd paid for the trip with her profits from the knitwear she'd sold, but after his reaction this morning when she'd talked to Cammie about him needing them, she decided not to. While she'd like to think he'd be proud she'd been doing so well, she was no longer certain.

"Look," he said, "I don't think I'd be very good company. I have things I need to take care of around the garage, and if I'm not doing them, I'll be distracted. Did you get an adjoining room for Matt and Cammie?"

"Yes, as always."

"It won't matter if I'm not there. Just cancel one room and the three of you can bunk together."

Susie knew that it made no sense to be angry since

she'd made these plans without consulting him. All the same, her frustration was becoming so sharp that it might as well be anger.

"It does matter because I planned this for all of us," she replied. "If you feel you can't be there, we'll just head on home, too."

Ben shook his head. "That's not fair to Matt and Cammie. I'm assuming they know about the trip?"

"Yes."

"Then take the time, build some memories with the kids and then come home rested and happy."

"That's what I'd been hoping for you," she replied.

"I appreciate that. Really. But you're just going to have to go on without me."

Which was exactly what Susie was beginning to fear.

CHAPTER FIVE

AFTER A MONDAY eaten up by travel and time change, Tuesday dawned no sunnier for Ben, who was having a breakfast meeting at the country club with Adriana Sanchez, his business manager. And, really, he was going to have to find a new venue for these breakfast meetings or he was going to start to connect this place to bad events, pretty much like he connected tequila to an overindulged twenty-first birthday.

"You're in a better position than many," Adriana said. "It just seems bleak because it's been so long since we've had a discussion about your overall financial picture. The quarterly review meetings I had asked for would have softened the blow."

Ben wasn't into second-guessing as a form of self-punishment. If he wanted to suffer, he'd order up his first shot of tequila in twenty years. Or he'd dwell upon the fact that today he could be out west, on Coronado Island with his family.

"I agree that the meetings would have been a good idea. From now on, I'll stay on top of that," he replied. "But let me ask you this…. If, as you tell me, my stock portfolio has rebounded to seventy percent of what it was worth before the market dropped, and if the acreage I hold outside of Charlotte is currently a break-even proposition at best, if I stopped being a driver tomorrow, could I keep everything afloat?"

Adriana was relatively young—somewhere in her early thirties, the best he could guess—but she was a graduate of one of the top business schools on the east coast and had spent a good number of years on Wall Street before opting for a simpler life and returning home to Mooresville. Ben trusted her judgment implicitly.

"You're too young to dip into your retirement accounts without paying a huge penalty," she said. "So I'm not even going to count those assets…which are considerable…as we discuss this."

"Okay," he replied.

"I've been trying to strike a balance for you, investing what is prudent, but keeping a reasonable cash reserve, even though you are well insured, should there be an accident that takes you off the track."

"Not quite the way I want to leave racing," he replied, earning a smile from this otherwise very serious young woman.

"That's good news," she said. "If you leave racing in a way that doesn't trigger insurance coverage but hypothetically don't bring in another penny from this minute forward…which you will…your available cash reserves would get you through approximately two years. Obviously, it will last longer if you make lifestyle adjustments and cut back on your donations. I'm sure you know you're beyond generous on that front."

"I've been lucky," he replied. "And for so long as I can continue to give at that level, I will."

His business manager's brown eyes warmed. "Which is one of the many reasons I like having you as a client."

"So what are my other options if I need to stretch it out longer than two years?"

"As you've mentioned, you have the stock portfolio and the land, though I wouldn't advise touching either of those right now."

"Anything else?"

"This conversation is wholly hypothetical, right?"

"Yes," Ben replied. At least he hoped like hell it was.

"Well, on a hypothetical level, you could always hole up on the family farm in Tennessee. That would be a far less expensive lifestyle."

Ben knew Adriana was joking, but he could work up only a weak smile. He had been a horrible farmer, and he'd gotten out the day he'd graduated from high school. Unlike his dad and his three brothers, he'd had no passion for it, had felt no connection to the land…or their hungry, demanding dairy herd. He'd been happy to buy more land for his brothers and help keep the place afloat just after his dad had died five years ago, but that was as close as he cared to be to Mother Earth at this point in his life.

Adriana laughed. "Based on your expression, you'd better keep your day job."

That's when it struck Ben—he might need his job, but at this moment, he didn't love it. And he wondered if he ever would again.

AT A CERTAIN AGE, children should be able to fly in the same airplane without the mother being subject to "Mom, he's looking out my window" or "Mom, she's hogging the armrest." Apparently, Matt and Cammie had not yet reached that milestone. Susie, who sat in the aisle seat next to the dueling duo, looked longingly across the way at the empty seat between two preoccupied businessmen. She supposed she might startle them if she clambered across the closest man and plopped down between them. Then again, if they'd turned even half an ear toward her children's general crabbiness, they might welcome her.

The days on Coronado's beach had been idyllic, as had been their stay in the vintage part of the sprawling hotel. Susie just wished Ben had been part of it, or that he would have at least taken a call from her. She'd finally gotten through to him at home last night, and he'd somewhat grudgingly agreed to pick them up at the airport today, but only after she'd told him she could always call a limo service.

"Ladies and gentlemen, we are now approaching Charlotte Douglas International Airport," announced a fuzzy voice over the loudspeaker at the same time Susie caught Matt making faces at Cammie. Susie gave her son a stern look, then checked her watch. It was nearly four in the afternoon, Charlotte time, but Susie was humming with pent-up energy after being on the plane for so very long. All she wanted to do was get home and settle in with Ben.

What felt like a lifetime later—but was probably only twenty minutes—Susie stood at the luggage carousel with Matt and Cammie waiting for their bags to appear. They were all waiting for Ben to appear, too. His text message just a moment ago had been a terse "Running late." That, Susie had already figured out.

"Here comes my suitcase," she said to Matt. "Let me grab it."

"I can get it, Mom," he said.

Except the bag was nearly as tall as him, and Susie could envision an end result of both Matt and the suitcase circling on the belt.

"Let me give you a hand," Ben said, seemingly appearing out of nowhere.

Susie watched as both of the males in her life retrieved the suitcase together.

"Sorry I wasn't here to greet you," her husband said once he'd placed the luggage next to her.

She came forward and gave him a quick kiss. "It doesn't matter. I'm just happy to see you now."

"Me, too."

Before he could help Cammie or Matt with their smaller suitcases, he was approached by a handful of autograph seekers. Ben was as gracious as ever, giving autographs and smiling as his picture was taken on every cell phone the group had. But as Susie looked at him, she grew a little sad. She knew it wasn't possible for a person to visibly age over the course of two days, but it seemed to her that Ben had. The lines radiating from the corners of his eyes appeared more pronounced and the set of his shoulders didn't have its usual military bearing.

"Mom, we've got our stuff," Cammie said from behind her.

"Dad's almost done," Susie absently replied as she reached for the handle on her suitcase and extended it.

"Ready?" Ben asked, taking her luggage from her. "I'm parked close by."

After only two more autograph stops, they were at the car. Ben had driven her SUV as opposed to his sleek sports car, which was made to accommodate neither luggage nor children. The ride home took place in silence, but more of the tired sort than the uncomfortable sort. That, Susie supposed, was progress.

After they'd pulled down the winding drive to their home, Ben didn't hit the button to open the garage door. Instead, he put the car in Park and sat with it idling.

"Can we get out?" Matt asked.

"Sure," Ben replied.

Before Susie could tell the kids to hang on and get their luggage, they were up and out.

"What's going on?" she asked Ben.

"I have someplace I have to be tonight. Don't expect me home until late."

She decided to try to keep things light. "That sounds highly mysterious. Are you moonlighting as a secret agent?"

"Nothing that exciting. Just a business meeting," Ben replied.

If he'd said he had to be at the track, Susie would have accepted the statement without a second thought. After all, tomorrow was qualifying day.

Recalling her vow to put it all out there, Susie said, "It seems odd to me that you'd have a business meeting when you're going to be at the track tomorrow. Usually, you're with Chris on Wednesday evening."

Ben gave her a level look. "Do I ask you about all the details of your day?"

"No, but I'd be happy to share them with you, if you did."

"I don't want to do that. We both deserve a level of privacy even though we're married." He glanced at the car's clock. "I'm going to be late. Can we save this discussion?"

Susie considered herself a patient woman, but she'd

just been pushed one dismissal too far. And like any good Tennessee-born girl, she knew that sweetness could be a thousand times sharper than vinegar.

"For when you get home…whenever that might be? Of course we can, honey. And you might as well just bring in all the luggage then, too. We wouldn't want to slow you down, now would we?"

She'd loaded the syrup heavier than Cammie did on French toast, and Ben was staring at her as though he'd never seen her before. Well, let him look! Susie exited the car and gave Ben an utterly false smile and very perky wave while sending a very different mental message: *Be as stubborn and secretive as you like, Benjamin Horatio Edmonds, but I am not backing down!*

But as she marched up the walk to her home's front door…

"Mom, I'm hungry," Cammie called from the kitchen as soon as Susie had entered the house.

"I'll order us pizza for dinner," Susie called back. Since the ordering of pizza was something that happened just about as often as Halley's Comet came around, that should buy some peace while she made a much-needed phone call.

"But I haven't even had lunch, and it's going to take forever to get pizza all the way out here," Cammie said from closer by.

Susie hesitated at the bottom of the oak circular staircase that led to their home's second floor and some measure of privacy for her. The child had a point. They lived so far outside town that pizza delivery required intense negotiations. And the snack boxes she'd let Cammie and Matt purchase on the plane had been amusing for their mini-playing cards and the mystery of hummus in a tube, but they'd hardly been a meal. In fact, they'd had no real meal today at all.

"Hang on, and we'll go fix something. But right now, I need to run upstairs. Grab a yogurt or something..." And then Susie dashed to her room before Cammie could catch her.

Once there, she closed the bedroom door, picked up the phone and dialed Maudie's Down Home Diner. Blessedly, Sheila Trueblood answered the phone.

"Sheila, it's Susie Edmonds."

"Hey, Susie, how was the California vacation?"

"Fine," Susie replied, knowing—or at least hoping— Sheila would get the real story later. And then she moved on to the purpose of her call. "Can you help me call an emergency meeting of the Tuesday Tarts for tonight?"

Sheila laughed. "So we're going to be the Wednesday Wenches?"

"Sure," Susie said. If she were in a happier mood, she might have smiled at Sheila's usual sharp wit. But Susie remained far from happy. "I know this is short notice, and that I'm asking a lot, but I need the counsel of wise women, and I can't think of any wiser."

"You know we're always here for each other," Maudie's owner replied. "How's nine o'clock?"

"Perfect," Susie replied. "And I'm bringing wine."

Sheila snorted. "Wine? You sound frazzled enough that I'm thinking of putting out a fifth of whiskey and a bunch of shot glasses."

"I just might take you up on that," Susie said grimly.

"I'll make the calls," Sheila said. "You just relax, and we'll see you in the back room at nine."

After she'd hung up the phone, Susie heaved a sigh of relief and flopped onto her bed. Thank heaven for tarts and wenches!

CHAPTER SIX

"THANKS FOR SEEING ME," Ben said to his friend Derek Garner, whom he'd just met up with in the most unlikely of locations—the indoor pool area at a Charlotte hotel. Both men sat poolside at a glass-topped table set in a circle of potted palms. Ben almost felt like the secret agent Susie had accused him of being.

"I wish it could be someplace with a little more decorum," Derek said inclining his head toward the pool where a group of about ten teenagers frolicked. Ben couldn't be precise about the number because they were moving around so quickly.

"The location isn't a problem," he said to Derek. "I'm just glad to find you're in town. Things have been crazy the past few weeks. I forgot you'd be here."

"You forgot after paying for all these kids to be at the races this weekend?" his friend asked. "You *do* have stuff going on."

Derek was a former NASCAR Nationwide Series driver and more recently the founder and executive director of Green Flag Racing, a day camp and supplemental education program for at-risk urban youth in Detroit. Ben had been a financial supporter for some time, and the work Derek was doing only got better with each passing year.

"Way too much stuff going on," Ben agreed. "But not much anyone who I can talk to about it."

Though he had dozens of friends here in North Carolina, most of them were still in the business. Ben needed to talk to someone whose NASCAR days were behind him.

"I'm here to listen," Derek said.

Ben cut to the chase. "How did you know when it was time for you to retire?"

If Derek was surprised by the question, he hid it well.

"I had things I wanted to do more than race," he replied. He paused a beat before asking, "So I take it that the R word has popped into your head?"

"It's more like it was surgically implanted there."

"If this is about retirement, I get why you're talking to me. It's not the kind of thing you want even whispered within the industry."

Ben nodded. "For sure. There's no guarantee I'll be with Double S Racing past this season and if the other teams think I'm considering retirement, they aren't going to take a serious look at me."

"Agreed," Derek said, then turned his attention to the pool. Using his fingers to send out an eardrum breaker of a whistle, he gained the kids' attention. "Time to bring it down a few hundred decibels."

Ben was damn impressed to see that not one of the kids so much as gave him the standard teen you're-so-boring look. Then he told the two counselors also watching the kids from poolside to get it in gear before they were all kicked to the curb.

"That's better," Derek said to Ben. "So who planted this retirement thing in your head?"

"First, I saw a couple of random posts on my fan site. Not exactly a call to retire, but more curiosity about how long I planned to continue racing. That, I could deal with. But after the California race last week, my crew chief pretty much volunteered me for retirement."

"Your crew chief? The new one…Chris Sampson?"

Ben nodded. "That would be the guy. We've clashed from the moment Gil dropped him into the middle of my team. I can do no right, and Sampson can do no wrong. Or at least he's that way in front of me. I've heard that he's less abrasive with others, which I have to believe because otherwise he'd be walking around with two black eyes on a daily basis."

Derek shook his head as though he hadn't heard right. "You haven't…?"

"No, we haven't fought, but I've been damn tempted."

"Then Sampson has to be a piece of work since you're one of the calmest guys I've ever met."

"Usually," Ben said. "But the farther I get into this season, the less I feel like myself. The friction Sampson is causing is a big part of it. He and I could use a session at your camp to get our teamwork skills in place. That, or a boxing ring. He's a chunk of years younger than I am, but I have life experience and a whole lot of anger on my side."

"Instead of twelve rounds, how about an arbitrator?" Derek asked.

Ben laughed.

"No, I mean it. You don't have to hire a professional if you don't want to, but if you sit down with a neutral third party, you might be able to work through some of this."

"I don't see it happening," Ben said.

"Just think about it, okay?"

"Okay."

Derek smiled. "Why don't I think you meant that?"

Ben laughed. "Because I'd sooner drive blindfolded than I'd go through something that sounds like marriage counseling with Chris Sampson."

"Consider the subject dropped," Derek said. "But once you do retire, whenever that might be, what are your plans?"

"That's number one on the Beats the Heck Out of Me list. I guess it always seemed so far in the future that I didn't need to think about it. And now here I am. Or potentially here I am."

"Other than driving, what do you like?" Derek asked.

Ben hitched this thumb toward the pool. "Being around kids, teaching them…learning from them. It's amazing what they can teach an adult about life."

Derek smiled. "I wish I could afford to have you on Green Flag's staff."

"Not a problem. You get me whenever you want me, for free. That's a promise."

Now Ben just needed to figure out who got him in exchange for a paycheck.

A FEW MINUTES BEFORE NINE that evening, Susie entered the front door of Maudie's Down Home Diner, carrying a bottle of red wine sheathed in a paper bag. She wasn't a whiskey woman, as Sheila had suggested, but tonight a glass of wine certainly sounded good.

As she walked through the diner's currently quiet public area, chat and laughter from the back room flowed toward her. Susie said hellos to the customers she knew, waved to the waitress and moved on to her friends. At least all was right in this part of the world. In the room, she found Sheila, Mellie, Patsy, Patsy's two daughters, Sophia and Grace, and Rue Larrabee, who had started the Tuesday Tarts' gathering and was the owner of the Cut 'N' Chat salon, located just a few doors down from Maudie's.

"So here you've gone and turned us into the Wednesday Wenches," Rue said. "So long as we can still be Tuesday Tarts, too, I'm all for it. The more estrogen I'm around, the better life looks."

Susie laughed, and even that simple action lightened her mood.

"Since you're swimming in estrogen at the salon, it has to be looking pretty darned rosy," she said.

"And don't forget that testosterone, either," Sheila said. "From where I'm sitting, you've been looking nearly delirious ever since the Tarts bought you Andrew in that bachelor auction."

Andrew Clark was now Rue's fiancé. The tarts had been in a frenzy of wedding planning since Rue had shared the news.

The stylist tipped back her head and let loose a laugh as big as her heart. "You might have bought him, but after that, the work was all mine!"

"I'd say the work was more his, the way you were backpedaling from him," Patsy added in.

As Susie listened to the loving banter, she took a corkscrew from the table Sheila always stocked with treats for nights such as this. After trimming away the bottle's foil, she twisted in the corkscrew and began to carefully draw the cork out.

"Bless it all!" she snapped when the cork did the exact same thing.

"What's wrong?" Sophia asked.

Susie held out the corkscrew. "I came off half corked."

Her friends laughed, and Sophia rose to join her at the treats table.

"Let me see that, and you go sit down," the younger woman said.

Susie was happy to hand over the wine. She took her usual spot right next to Patsy on the loveseat and settled in.

"And speaking of romance," Patsy said to Sheila, who was kicked back in a fat armchair, a glass of whiskey, neat, in her hand. "What's going on with you and Gil Sizemore?"

"What do you mean, what's going on? I've told you all over and over, he's a diner customer just like any other," Sheila replied in a tone Susie would almost peg as alarmed.

"Oh, I'll agree he's a customer, but most of your customers don't look at you the way he does."

"And just how do you think the man looks at me?" Sheila asked.

"Judging by what I saw at lunch today, he looks at you like you're the best thing since sweet tea," Patsy said.

"He does not!"

"I don't know, Sheila. Mom's right," Sophia said as she poured Susie's wine into one of the diner's tumblers. "I've caught him looking your way a time or two, and I'd have to agree the man's sweet on you."

"I'd advise both of you to skip the wine," Sheila replied. "You're already not seeing clearly. Gil is a valued customer and nothing more. Just because a man says hello and might talk to a woman for a while doesn't mean he's sweet on her."

"It does if he watches her every time she's not looking," Susie said after thanking Sophia for the wine she'd brought her.

"Not you, too?" Sheila said. "I'm beginning to think it's something in the water in this town. Do all of you have vision problems? Gil Sizemore could not possibly be checking me out."

"I can guarantee my vision's 20/20, or I wouldn't be working on any of your heads, and I've got to say I've seen you watching Gil, too, Sheila," Rue announced.

The diner owner had blushed as red as her fiery hair. "I have not! Gil Sizemore isn't my type at all. He's all smooth and glossy and polished. He might as well have been dipped into varnish!"

"Un-huh. Right," Rue said, one perfectly plucked eyebrow arched with skepticism.

"Me thinks the lady doth protest too much," Susie added.

Sophia handed Patsy a glass of wine, then took a seat in the chair next to Sheila's. "I'm going to stay out of this since my mom told me to mind my own business, but if I were to jump in…," she added with her perpetually serious expression in place, "I'd have to agree."

"Thanks for *almost* staying out of it," Sheila said to her friend in a teasing voice. "It's a good thing I adore you, isn't it?"

Sophia smiled in return.

"And not just to save myself from further speculation, but because she's the reason we're here tonight, would you like to tell us what's happened, Susie?"

With all this talk of crushes and new love, it felt more than a little odd to be talking about what she feared was fading love, but Susie had no place else to turn.

"I don't suppose there's any good place to start this," she said. "I've always kept my own counsel when it comes to my marriage. Ben's been my very best friend since the day we met, and I've always been able to talk to him."

Her friends nodded in understanding, and Susie tried to relax. "Except…except lately, every time I try to talk to him about something of more substance than where the kids and I have to be or if the trash has been put out, he bolts from the room…or the state."

"What do you mean?" Sheila asked.

"Well, you know when you asked me how the California trip was?"

"Yes."

"I omitted one thing. I had tried to get Ben to stay with me and the kids on Coronado Island for a few days of R & R, but he refused. He told me he had things to take care of back here, and really, it's more the way he said it than the words themselves."

"You saw firsthand what I went through when Dean and I separated," Patsy said. "You know I understand. But it *is* the season. You have to give him a little leeway for that."

"I know, and if it were just that, I wouldn't have asked Sheila to get you all together."

"So what else has happened?" Rue asked.

"It all sounds silly when looked at as a single incident, but when I put it all together, it doesn't seem so silly."

"Give us a 'for instance,'" Patsy requested.

Susie took a sip of wine and then replied, "Well, for instance, he was late to the airport to pick us up this afternoon, which never happens. Then when we got home, he more or less dumped us in the driveway before taking off." She gave a small shake of her head. "I swear the tires squealed. And worst of all, before I got out of the truck, when I asked him where he was going, he refused to tell me."

"Refused?" asked Sheila. "That's a strong word."

Susie nodded. "I know. He told me that he doesn't ask what I do all day long, so I shouldn't do that to him. Except I don't. I just wanted to know what the big rush was this evening."

She looked around the room, wondering if she could work up the courage to ask the question that had formed in her mind as she'd sat next to Ben in their own driveway and watched the geography of her world shift.

"Do you think it's possible that he's seeing someone?"

"You mean like a chiropractor?" Rue asked.

"No, I mean like a mistress."

Rue laughed. "No, really. Ben, of all people?"

"I'm serious," Susie replied. "After the way he behaved tonight, it's something I need to consider. And it's possible, too. For the first time since we married, he's been on the road without me. I know he wasn't fully behind the choice we made for the kids' sake, and I know he's been lonely and stressed over how poorly he's been doing."

"And so you think he could be having an affair?" Patsy asked.

Susie nodded.

The group sat silent for a moment, deliberating. Susie took another sip of wine to mask her nervousness.

"I'm not seeing this," Sheila finally said. "What in blue blazes would make you think Ben would be unfaithful just because he's not happy with his racing? Because as much as y'all have been watching me, I've been returning the favor. I've seen the two of you in here for lunch enough times that I can tell you point-blank that Ben Edmonds is crazy in love with you."

Patsy nodded. "Ben's an honorable man. He'd never do something like that, no matter how unhappy he might be with his career circumstances. And he's so much more than just a driver, too. He supports charities, volunteers his time all over the place and mentors the rookie drivers. That's not the kind of man who skulks about with another woman."

Susie sighed. "Okay, maybe. But there have been other instances of people leading secret lives."

"I know it's happened, but not with your husband," Patsy replied. "From what Dean says, Ben turns beet-red when he tries to bluff at poker. I think you're just too close to the situation to see it clearly."

"I could be. It's tough to be objective when your husband goes all silent on you." Susie could feel her own color rising at even the thought of what she needed to share next. But she needed to do this for both her and Ben. "There's one more thing. Our love life isn't what it used to be. In fact, it's virtually nonexistent. He's always too tired, or the kids are giving us trouble, or..." She trailed off and shrugged her shoulders. "It just isn't happening."

"Midlife crisis," Rue said firmly. "Men really get into that."

"A midlife crisis *now?*" Susie asked. "It seems so early."

"You're, what, forty? I know this because I brought the cake that Tuesday night," Rue said. "And Ben's close to the same age, right?"

"Yes?"

"Then when do you think a midlife crisis might come into the picture?" Rue asked.

"Maybe when we're fifty-five or so?"

Patsy laughed. "So you're planning to live to be one hundred and ten?"

Susie had to laugh, too, when she considered the math.

"Absolutely," she replied.

"So, ladies, we agree that a midlife crisis could be at play here?" Rue asked the gathering.

Everyone but Mellie nodded.

"You're a little out of my league on this. What would be the signs?" the normally quiet woman asked.

"If Ben weren't a NASCAR driver, I'd say suddenly buying a motorcycle or a hot sports car, but these guys did that as soon as they had two nickels to rub together," Patsy said.

"There's always the new haircut," Sheila offered. "Or worse yet, they grow a weird little goatee."

"Ben doesn't have those," Mellie said.

"And then there's the sudden silences and the inattentiveness to the wife," Rue added.

"Which Ben has been doing," Susie said.

"And the mysterious behavior as he tries to grab back youth," Sheila said.

Susie sighed.

"Midlife crisis," Patsy confirmed. "But at least you know what you're dealing with."

"But what's the solution? Old age?" Susie asked, feeling somewhere south of glum.

"No, the solution is to spice it up. You need to bring pizzazz back into Ben's life," Patsy said.

"Pizzazz," Susie repeated. "I don't know that we had pizzazz back before we had Cammie and Matt."

"Sure you did!" Rue exclaimed. "What's the craziest place you ever made love?"

A memory came back to Susie, one so hot that she nearly needed to fan herself.

"I'm not sharing that information, but I'll admit we had pizzazz," she told the Tarts.

"Get it back, woman!" Rue cried.

Then the Tarts did what they did best, and set to planning.

CHAPTER SEVEN

QUALIFYING DAY held a mathematical simplicity that appealed to Ben. Charlotte equaled a maximum of two laps around a 1.5-mile oval track, the frontstretch longer than the backstretch, Turns Three and Four shorter than One and Two. Drive fast, qualify well. Drive slow, bring up the rear. He wished the rest of life could be broken down into such basic components. Maybe it could, and he just wasn't seeing the patterns. The one pattern he clearly sensed at this moment, though, was that of he and Chris Sampson circling each other like angry badgers.

Prequalifying practice done, Ben and Chris stood on opposite sides of the No. 515 car, which rested in its garage. The crew was beginning basic work to tweak it before tonight's qualifying laps. Chris had, as usual, issued orders in terse phrases of as few words as possible, and wasn't otherwise communicating with the team's two mechanics.

"Anything else other than the vibration you noticed in the final lap?" Sampson asked Ben without looking up from his clipboard.

"No." *Or I would have mentioned it.*

"The car checked out fine this morning."

Had it been any other person, Ben would have put the comment down to idle chat during troubleshooting. Not so with his crew chief.

"I'm sure it did," he said. "All I'm saying is that now you need to have this issue checked out."

"And all I'm saying is that I heard you the first time."

Ben glanced at the two mechanics, who stood at the front of the car with the hood up. Both looked pretty much like they wanted to crawl in with the engine.

"Chris, step outside with me," he said, making it clear this was a demand and not a request.

"No time," Sampson replied.

"Problem, gentlemen?" asked a voice from the back of the car.

Both Ben and Chris turned to see Gil Sizemore standing there.

"No problem here," Sampson said.

"Big one here," Ben replied.

Gil hitched his thumb toward the garage's open door. "Let's take a walk, Ben."

Ben wasn't sure where this was going to get him, but anyplace had to be better than where he was.

"I take you and Chris haven't come up with some sort of working arrangement?" Gil asked as they walked down the long row of garage stalls.

"We have…just not the same one," Ben replied.

"It's affecting your focus," Gil said. "That's clear to all of us."

"He's no Steve Benedict," Ben said, referring to his former crew chief.

"I know. And I know that you and Steve had been together eight years…half your NASCAR career. I like Steve, but it was time to split you two up. You'd grown stagnant."

"I like to think of it as comfortable."

"Comfortable is when you're consistently in the Chase. It's not when you're no longer making the Chase."

Ben couldn't argue with that.

"Look, Ben, I agree this has been tough, but it's my team and I have to make decisions that will benefit everyone. Chris is hungry," Gil said. "He knows that his future hinges on how well this team does."

"That holds true for all of us," Ben replied. "But the rest of us have been around the track enough times to know that success comes from unity, not creating divided loyalties."

"And you think he does that?"

"He treats me with a lack of respect in front of the rest of the team. He could do less harm by jamming a screwdriver into the car's gearbox."

Gil kept silent, and if Ben really gave a damn about his future, maybe he should do the same. But he applied a little math to this situation, and it came out damned if he spoke and damned if he didn't. He opted to speak.

"Look, I know I'm walking a thin line with Double S these days, so I've kept my mouth shut. But here's how Sampson's arrival has been playing out for me. You fire the guy who's been my closest coworker for half my career and then bring in his replacement without consulting me. It's your team, your choices, and I understand and usually appreciate the way you manage. Not this time, though."

Gil stopped walking, so Ben did, too.

"So what you're telling me is that we have a difference of opinion regarding my choice of Chris Sampson."

"Yes," Ben replied.

"And you understand Chris is here to stay."

"Yes."

"As you said, my team, my choices. And I make them to win. Given that all of this is fact, what do you propose to do?" Gil asked.

"Same thing as always. Race to win."

Double S's owner nodded. "That's a good start."

And a good ending to a career, too, Ben thought.

By Friday evening, Susie was sure of one thing: she should have read more issues of *Cosmo*. Okay, maybe she should have read even one issue. Or attended a school for seductresses, if there was such a thing.

"And if there isn't, there should be," she said to her reflection in her dressing room mirror. If there were, Susie feared she'd be in the running for class clown.

Rue sold a wonderful line of cosmetics at the salon, but her friend's enthusiasm while doing her makeup had led to a heavy hand. And before that, Susie had been waxed, pedicured, shampooed and styled to within an inch of her life. Since she was far more a nature girl than the primp-and-perfume sort, she'd left the salon suffering from sensory overload.

Add to that craziness an afternoon spent talking business and scheduling a Monday appointment with boutique chain owner Martine Roulot, getting Matt to soccer, Cammie to her riding lesson, and both of them through their homework before they went to the Grosso farm for an overnight. In theory, Cammie was there to babysit for little Lily, who Mellie had allowed to become part of the Tarts' plans, and Matt to help Patsy set up the video game system she'd purchased.

The scheme was a little convoluted, yes, but it was better than having to inform her children that she needed them gone for the evening in order to have her way with their father. Heaven knew it was times like these that Susie wished for blood family who lived closer, instead of them all being in Tennessee. But her NASCAR family had become as close as kin, as their efforts on her behalf tonight proved.

Susie turned away from the mirror before she chickened out, wiped off the makeup, slipped out of the four inch high heels, and put the "barely there" pale blue silk dress Patsy had found her back on its hanger. She walked out of the dressing room on wobbly ankles as her stilettos sunk into the thick ivory carpet. There was a reason she wore flats 99.9% of the time, and this was it. Nothing was seductive about an ankle sprain. Many mincing steps later, she settled into her armchair in front of the bedroom fireplace. There, at least she had her knitting to distract her until Ben arrived home.

Susie pulled out the bell sleeve for a royal blue mohair holiday sweater she'd started work on earlier in the week. In time, the steady rhythm of her knitting soothed her… right until she heard the sound of the motion sensor by the back door chiming, and then Ben's familiar footsteps on the floor below. She set aside her work and made her miraculously injury-free way to the top of the stairs.

"I'm home," Ben called, though she couldn't see him yet.

Susie felt just a tad too Scarlett O'Hara standing at the top of the circular staircase, but the Tarts had insisted that the most dramatic start to the evening would be if he saw her there.

"I'm upstairs," she called.

Ben appeared from the hallway that led toward the den and then the kitchen.

"Hi," she said for lack of a sexier greeting.

Ben just stood there for about five of Susie's heart-beats, each of which echoed strongly in her ears.

"Are we going out?" he finally asked. "Did I forget about a sponsor cocktail party?" He reached into his pocket and pulled out his phone, on which he always kept his schedule.

"No, we're home for the evening," she replied. "Why don't you go on into the den?"

"Where are the kids?" Ben looked around as though they might materialize from thin air.

"They're having an overnight."

"Oh." Still appearing vaguely lost, he ran his hand though his hair. "So…I don't need to get changed or put on a tie or anything?"

"No, you're wonderful the way you are. Go on into the den. I'll be right there." She preferred that there be no witness as she teetered her way downstairs with a white-knuckle grip on the handrail.

When Susie arrived in the den, her husband stood in the middle of the room, again looking like a stranger in a strange land. She had gathered all the memorabilia she could from their first trip to New York City sixteen years earlier, when Ben's Rookie of the Year honors had been celebrated at NASCAR's annual banquet. Those had been heady times, both for Ben and for them as a couple.

"Champagne?" she offered.

"Sure," Ben replied, then wandered to the mantel, which she'd adorned with photos of the two of them from that banquet night. She'd been wearing a dress the color of the one she had on now, but it had been much more conservative in cut and fabric. He hadn't been able to keep his eyes off her that night. Tonight, not so much.

Susie removed the foil and wire cage from the champagne and set them on the cocktail table in front of the sofa, where two glasses also waited. Keeping Patsy's advice of "turn the bottle, not the cork" well in mind due to the hefty price tag on the bubbly, Susie opened it and was rewarded with a sharp *pop*. Once she'd filled two glasses, she handed one to Ben.

"This is the same champagne we had that night," she said.

He took a sip. Susie watched as he tried—and failed—to hide a grimace.

"You don't like it?" she asked.

"It's just hitting the bottom of an empty stomach pretty hard." He sat in a wingback chair perpendicular to the much more couples-friendly sofa. "It's been a long day. I'm whipped."

Clearly, she was at the bottom of the bell curve when it came to seduction school grades. She needed to regroup. "I have some appetizers. Should I go get them?"

"That would be great," he said in a slow and sleepy voice.

"Okay, then." Susie headed to the den's door and considered making her next stop the hills.

"And babe?"

She turned back.

"You look pretty."

"Thank you," Susie replied. She'd been shooting for too sexy to survive, but okay.

A couple of minutes later, she returned to the den with a tray of hors d'oeuvres that came fairly close to what they'd had that night in New York City. She'd kept that night in her memory for so long: Ben's joy at what he'd attained, the magical feeling she'd had of being transported into a dream and the passion they'd later shared.

Susie set the tray on the cocktail table.

Ben sat up and took a spear of asparagus wrapped in a ribbon of paper thin smoked salmon.

"Fancy, but good."

"Do you remember having this before?" she asked.

"Nope, but I like it," he said, reaching for another one. "Hey, did I mention that I qualified tenth again? Second race in a row."

"Fancy that," she said, wondering if she should just plop herself down in his lap while holding his Rookie of the Year trophy. Maybe one or the other of them would earn his full attention.

Ben took another sip of his champagne. "Better now. I like the way it tastes with the salmon."

Susie tried again. "Remember how it tasted with strawberries and whipped cream?" *In bed.*

"Have I had this before?" he asked, then glanced at the bottle. "You'd think I'd remember a fancy bottle all painted up with flowers."

"Yes, you would. Does none of this seem the least bit familiar to you?" she asked. "The champagne, the awards program, the food?" Her irritation had gone from simmer to a full boil. *"The color of this dress?"*

"It matches your eyes," he said. "Is there something else I'm missing?"

There was, and she wasn't sure at whose feet the blame lay.

"Really?" he asked blankly. "I just thought you'd decided to redecorate the den a little."

She gestured at her dress. "You think I'd redecorate the den in *this?*"

"I don't know, honey. Maybe it makes the housework more fun?"

Susie finally snapped. "Oh, for heaven's sake! I'm trying to seduce you, Ben. And clearly I'm not doing a very good job if you can't figure that out."

Ben rose and moved toward her. "Honey, I knew what you were doing the second I saw you at the top of those stairs. What red-blooded man wouldn't?"

He drew her into his arms. Torn between laughter and annoyance, she made a token effort to push him away.

"You tease!"

"Takes one to know one, right?"

Susie gave in to the laughter. "I guess it does, Ben Edmonds."

How had she missed that he was teasing her? Granted, it had been a long time since he'd been this free and fun, but she shouldn't have missed the way even now the sides of his mouth twitched as he worked to hold in a smile. And she should hardly have overlooked the lights that danced in his hazel eyes.

"I remember it all, sweet Susie. I remember the way you looked in that pretty blue dress…almost exactly the color of this one. I remember the way you cried when I accepted my award. I remember the way I told myself that night I'd fight to hand you the world."

Susie could feel those tears starting again. She'd been so proud of him that she simply hadn't been able to contain it.

He kissed her once, twice…brief tastes that whetted her appetite for more.

"That night, I wanted you so much, we barely made it to our room, remember?" he asked.

Susie felt almost drugged by the pressure of his body against hers, the touch of his lips against the sensitive skin of her neck. *Remember? It was happening all over again!*

This time he kissed her deeply, with total, delicious attention to her.

"You'd better grab that champagne and take off those man-killer shoes," he said.

She blinked. "Why?"

"Because it's about to be winner take all when I chase you up the stairs and straight to our room. I wouldn't want you to be at too much of a disadvantage."

Laughing, Susie twined her arms around her husband's neck.

"I'll get the champagne but I'm leaving the shoes on," she said.

His smile was slow and sexy enough to make Susie's heart skip.

"Really? Why?" he asked.

"Because you can have it all…."

NIGHT WAS JUST BEGINNING to give way to the first light of dawn. Eyes blurry, mind scarcely awake, Susie stretched and savored the delicious feeling of relaxation that lingered in the wake of last night's lovemaking. Maybe they hadn't talked, but they had reestablished an intimacy that had been lacking for far too long. Last night had reminded Susie of one central truth—Ben and she loved each other.

She reached for him, wanting his warmth all over again, but his side of the bed was empty.

Susie sat up. "Ben?"

"Over here," he said quietly.

Focusing a little more, she made out his silhouette at the window. He'd drawn open the drapes and was standing there in his robe. What he could be looking at in the scant light, she had no idea.

"It's early yet. Why don't you come back to bed?" she suggested.

"Maybe in a minute," he replied.

"Okay," she replied and settled back in.

The sky grew lighter and yet Susie's bed was empty.

"What are you thinking about?" she asked her husband.

"Nothing," he replied.

It was a lie, yet not one she chose to call him on. Last night had been good, but they weren't back on track yet.

CHAPTER EIGHT

"G<small>REAT WORK</small>, Ben."

Ben grinned as he listened to his crew chief's words come through the two-way radio wired into his helmet.

"What did you say, Chris? I'm not sure I caught that."

"I said great work."

Damn right it was. Ben had just fought his way back from being tangled up in an accident to take ninth in the Charlotte race. Not only was it his best finish of the year, but he couldn't think of a single time that either reflexes or hesitation had impeded him. He didn't feel like a new man, but he didn't feel like such an old man, either.

"Thanks, Chris," he said. "Couldn't have done it without you."

"Right," the younger man replied.

Ben chose to take that as "Right, and we couldn't have done it without you, either." He would not let the crew chief's lack of interpersonal skills kill his joy.

And tonight he'd do the seducing of Susie.

After Ben had exited the car and shared his praise for a job well done with the rest of the team, he walked over to where Kane, his agent, stood at the fringes of a cluster of well-wishers.

Kane held out his hand to Ben. "Damn good job. Exactly what we need to keep seeing from you."

"That's what I plan to deliver," he said. If they were anywhere but in the middle of a sea of industry people, he would have added, "For so long as I have a job."

"Walk over this way with me," Kane said.

Ben nodded.

"There's another glitch in the sponsor situation," Kane said in a low voice once they were out of earshot from everyone else. "Hometeam Insurance has told Double S that they're willing to stay as a sponsor, but only if their logos are on another car."

"They're trying to force me out? What the hell's the point of that?"

"I don't know. I've heard they have a new advertising agency and it could have something to do with that. Maybe they're not looking for the same image."

Ben shook his head. "Yeah, because safe and professional is such a bad image for an insurance company," he replied with no small amount of sarcasm.

"Look, you just keep driving like you did tonight, and I'm going to make some contacts inside Hometeam. I just wanted you to know the latest developments before you heard them from Gil."

"Thanks," Ben said, wondering how a night that started out so right could end up so wrong.

MONDAY MORNING at 10:45, Susie stepped across the threshold of La Vie, Charlotte's hottest new upscale women's clothing boutique. Susie had loved the shop long before one arrived in North Carolina, having visited branches in the Caribbean and France when the family took its annual vacation at the end of the NASCAR

Sprint Cup season. The thought of having her designs actually sold in a place this posh floored her, but it could well happen. In fifteen minutes she had an appointment with the chain's owner, Martine Roulot.

Susie had spoken to Martine a number of times on the phone, and had a mental image of a Frenchwoman with the flair of Coco Chanel, the figure of a supermodel and the IQ of a genius. Clearly, the flair part was true. Like its sister stores, this one carried a mix of ready-to-wear from big designers and "one-offs" created by people like Susie. Vintage jewelry mixed with new, and European sensibilities with American. Billie Holiday's unmistakably poignant voice played softly in the background, transporting the shopper to another era. A retail experience could get no better than this. Even if Susie didn't work out an arrangement with Martine, her credit card would be getting quite a workout.

Enthralled, Susie wandered from rack to rack and then on to an antique secretary filled with vintage brooches. Susie's soft spot was vintage buttons bought to give special detail to her sweaters, but she could see adding brooches to her stockpile.

She'd just turned away from the secretary when she saw a young saleswoman with an elfin face and short-cropped hair fussing with a mannequin. She said hello, and the younger woman inclined her head politely. If this were Susie's store, she'd insist the staff give a verbal greeting, but perhaps the idea was to let the customer ease into the shopping experience. Then Susie checked her watch. She'd definitely eased in; her appointment time had arrived without her even noting the passage of time.

"Excuse me, I have an appointment with Martine

Roulot," she said to the saleswoman who was now rear-ranging a scarf on the mannequin's neck. "Can you tell me where I might find her?"

"I am Martine," the woman replied. Her French accent was lovely and exotic to Susie. "And you are Susie Edmonds."

Susie smiled. No wonder Martine hadn't spoken; Susie would have recognized that distinctive voice anywhere.

"I am."

"I hope you'll forgive me for my little game…not speaking when you came into the store, but I knew who you were."

"How?" Susie asked, startled.

"The internet is a powerful and interesting tool, is it not? And when one is married to a race car driver, it seems that one's picture is everywhere, *non?*"

Susie winced a little. "Believe me, I wish it weren't." Nine times out of ten, when she checked out those shots, Susie saw something a little Zombie-like in her eyes. She detested having her picture taken, but as Martine had said, it was to be expected.

The Frenchwoman gave a classically Gallic shrug. "Revel in it…and always wear one of your works. Free publicity is the very best kind."

"Point taken," Susie said.

Martine held out her hand. "And now, let's become official businesswomen."

They shook hands, and Susie said, "Thank you for taking the time to see me."

"How could I resist? You have piqued my curiosity since I saw some of your summer shells in a shop while I was scouting a location for La Vie. You are an artist."

"Not really," Susie replied. "I just knit a little."

Martine made a flicking motion with her right hand. "It's far more than that. I've been watching you, the way you touched the silks, the sigh of pleasure when you ran your hand against the cashmere shawl. And as for the way you rearranged my jewelry case, you have an eye for color and balance."

"I rearranged your jewelry?" Susie hurried over to the antique secretary. She had, indeed.

"It was entirely unconscious of me," she told Martine. "Sometimes it just happens." Sheila teased her when she did it at Maudie's, too.

"Lucky for us both I like the arrangement. Now let me get Colleen from the stock room, and you and I shall go back into the office and talk about what we can do for each other."

Though she was far too short to be a runway model, Martine moved with all the smooth speed and grace of one. She was gone in the blink of an eye and back before Susie could fall in love with any more merchandise.

The boutique's back office was the same as many Susie had seen, small and filled with samples and swatches and bits of bric-a-brac waiting to be used in displays.

"Please have a seat," Martine said, gesturing at an antique chair Susie wagered often did double duty as part of a display on the shop floor.

Susie sat and placed her purse on the floor next to her.

"As we have discussed on the phone, I would like to carry your merchandise," Martine said. "But as we have also discussed, I have some concerns that you will not be able to fill my orders. I believe that my customers will be clamoring for much from you, and my rule is never to disappoint a customer. That means I don't carry your work unless I'm sure you can deliver."

"I know I've been small-scale, but I do have two knitters who do piecework for me when I fall behind," Susie said. "If you can give me a good estimate of the number of pieces you think you want, I'll have a better sense if I can accommodate you."

The Frenchwoman gave a number that made Susie feel like she'd just started down a roller coaster's biggest hill.

When her stomach returned to its proper place, she asked, "Winter pieces for next year?"

"Non," Martine replied. "I would want to start with your summer shells and shrugs. What we are talking about, Susie, is a large step, but it's also a natural progression. Do you not want to see more women wearing your designs? Do you not want to know just how far you can go in business?"

For years, she had been Ben's wife, Ben's support system, and for years that had been enough. But since she'd been home this season, she'd begun to wonder what she could build for herself. One of the things she and Ben held in common was that competitive spark. Maybe it was time to let hers grow to a full light. Ben would support her in this; it was only fair.

"Yes, I do want all of that," she said to Martine. "I just have to figure out how to do it."

"I would be happy to help you through the process, especially since it is to my customers' benefit that you do this," the Frenchwoman added with a quick flash of a smile.

"I'd love your advice. Thank you," Susie replied.

Martine's laugh was low and husky. "You will not thank me so much when you're in the middle of the craziness this business can bring."

But crazy, Susie knew. She'd already been on one wild ride with Ben.

"I'M GOING TO DRIVE to Martinsville today," Ben said to Susie on Wednesday morning as they had an early morning cup of coffee before the kids rose.

Ben was actually looking forward to the drive. The track for the weekend's race was less than two hours from home, and he could use the time alone. Driving, both competitively and for leisure, cleared his head of the extraneous noise in life. Even after the good showing at Charlotte, he was hearing a lot of it.

"Can't you hold off until tomorrow morning? Qualifying is on Friday, right?" his wife asked.

"It is, but Kane and I have a dinner planned for tonight with executives from Hometeam Insurance."

Susie would take this dinner as "business as usual" when it remained anything but. Kane had gotten Ben the audience he needed, though. If the relationship was to be saved, it would have to be on a personal level instead of being driven by faceless consultants and outside contractors.

"Okay, I understand," Susie said. "I'd like to schedule a meeting for Monday with Adriana Sanchez. And I want both of us to be there."

Ben would have been less surprised if she'd said she wanted to schedule a joint session of Congress. She'd never asked to meet with their business manager. And right now wasn't particularly a time he wanted this to pop up. He'd worked hard to keep Susie insulated from his money stress.

"No need. I just saw her a few weeks ago, and things are under control," he replied, marveling how easily that lie came to him.

"I'd still like the appointment."

"Why?"

She frowned at his question but answered nonetheless.

"It's time that I learn more about money and investments. It seems I'm going to need to borrow a little from our nest egg to expand my business."

Ben's stomach tightened. He didn't want to see their available cash depleted just now.

"Expand, how?" he asked. "There's just one of you, and you're naturally limited by the hours in a day, right?"

Susie hesitated, then said, "Actually, for the past several months there's been more like three of me. I've been hiring a couple of knitters on a contract basis to help me fill my orders. Now I'm going to need about thirty more people since La Vie is going to be carrying my work. Martine thought I should just contract overseas, but there are plenty of women around here who can knit and are also looking for jobs. Eventually, I think it would make a great program to train new knitters from low-income areas in North Carolina and give them a chance to—"

"Whoa, there," Ben said, putting the brakes on whatever she'd planned to say next. "La Vie…Martine…. I have no idea what you're talking about."

"Martine Roulot owns a chain of boutiques called La Vie. At first they were located exclusively in resort towns, but now she's branching out. Remember the call I took while we were in California?"

"The one you held in the motor home's bathroom? Yes."

Susie nodded. "That call was Martine. We've been talking in a general way about my designs since then, and we met at her new shop in Charlotte on Monday. I thought she'd be offering to put my sweaters in the Charlotte store, but she wants them everywhere." A bemused expression on her face, Susie shook her head. "Twenty-five boutiques around the world. Can you believe it?"

Her excitement was so obvious. It would be cruel and wrong to talk her out of pursuing this even though it would take some heat off him financially and otherwise. But this was her dream, and he recalled how it felt to have one.

"It sounds great," he said with as much enthusiasm as he could muster. "How much do you think you're going to need in start-up money?"

"I don't know," she replied. "Probably in the range of thirty thousand."

"Wow. We definitely don't have that much in the dressing room coin jar."

"No, we don't. And the thirty is on top of the ten thousand in profits I've saved over the past year. But this is one of the reasons I want to meet with Adriana. I need her input on how much capital to have on hand. And I need your approval, too. I won't take this step without it."

"I am," he said. "One hundred percent."

Susie's face lit up. "Thank you! I knew I could count on you to be on board."

On board?

Ben felt as though he was about to walk the plank.

CHAPTER NINE

MARTINSVILLE TURNED OUT TO BE one fine slice of hell. Ben had qualified well at sixth, but then had been taken out of serious contention. First, there had been a botched pit stop early in the race, but he might have been able to come back from that if fate hadn't messed with him, too.

The field had run under three caution flags for minor accidents, which meant he couldn't advance for any of those laps. But the final blow had been in lap 448. While they were under the third yellow flag, despite Ben's strongly worded suggestions, Chris hadn't let him pit for fresh tires, and those behind him in the field then did. Once the caution was lifted, Ben's competitors had blown away the No. 515 car with their superior grip on the track. Bottom line: a forty-first place finish stunk.

Ben was at his car stowing the last of his gear and preparing for the drive home when his crew chief approached.

"Talladega will be better," Chris said.

"It couldn't get much worse," Ben replied.

Sampson's face looked grim and shadowed under the parking lot's lighting. "I made some poor judgments today," he said. "I won't do that next week."

The problem was, Ben didn't even care about Talladega and that had always been one of his favorite race venues—fast and fun. He closed his car's trunk with a firm hand.

"I don't want or expect an apology from you," Ben said. "But just so we're clear on this, it's not the risk you took that was the poor judgment. It was not listening to me when I tried to tell you that was the time to pit. I have sixteen years of Sprint Cup Series experience. When I said I knew the guys behind me were going to pit, I was saying it because I know them. I know their patterns and I know how they race. You're smart, Chris, but this is a team sport, and whether it's with me or another driver, you're not going to find success until you grasp that."

Sampson didn't say anything back, and in a way, that was progress, Ben supposed. But he just didn't care about Chris anymore, either. This evening's race had left Ben clean tapped out of give-a-damn.

"I have a two-hour drive in front of me," he said. "And tomorrow I'm going to…I don't know…go fishing or whatever the hell I feel like that doesn't involve work. I'll be back to the shop when I'm ready, so Chris, don't call me, I'll call you."

And then Ben got in his car and began to drive. The question that remained was where he'd end up.

SUSIE DIDN'T BELIEVE in divorce, but she was rethinking her position on murder. Yes, last night Ben had called to let her know that he was tired and stopping at a hotel to catch some sleep. No, he hadn't told her that he would not be attending the meeting with Adriana Sanchez this morning. And that was feeling very much like a capital offense to Susie.

She had tried reaching him at least a dozen times while she had sat alone in a conference room at Adriana's office. She'd felt like a fool, both for not knowing where her husband was and for having assumed he would show up. In the end, she'd apologized to Adriana, canceled the meeting, gone home and had a good long cry. Once the tears had been tapped out, anger had settled in. And some good fantasies had arrived, too; Ben staked to the ground over a fire anthill with honey poured on him and a pack of grizzlies circling had been her favorite.

Now that it was nearly time to go pick up Matt and Cammie from school, Susie's anger had again cycled its way back toward worry. She was in the kitchen, phone in hand to call over to Double S, just in case he'd checked in there, when she heard the sound of the garage door rising.

The prodigal spouse had returned.

"I'm glad to see that you're okay," Susie said from her spot at the kitchen table when Ben came into the house. Actually, he looked worn and weary, but whatever was bothering him right now would seem a trifle by the time she was through with him.

"Where have you been?" she asked.

"I needed some time to clear my head," he replied as he set down the leather duffel bag she'd gotten him for his last birthday. He made no move to join her at the table, though.

"Apparently, the head-clearing worked since you totally forgot to show up at Adriana's office this morning. You can't have missed all of my messages."

"I got them," he admitted.

His words were a blow to her heart. Maybe she hadn't cried herself out, after all. But she'd be damned if she'd cry in front of him.

"I guess I'll give you credit for not making up some

broken cell phone excuse," she said. "But in all the years we've known each other, you've never treated me with such total disrespect. How could you do that, Ben? How could you leave me sitting there, waiting for you, when you had no intention of showing up? You hurt me. Truly, deeply hurt me."

He didn't answer immediately.

"I should have called you when I knew I wasn't going to make it there, I agree," he eventually said. "And I'm sorry for that. But it's not that big of a deal. I wasn't critical to the discussion, and I had already told you that I support you."

"Easy words when you don't back them up with the least effort," she replied, unable to keep her pain from her voice. "What I got from you this morning had nothing to do with support. And for what it's worth, there were no discussions with Adriana. After sitting there and waiting for you like that, I was too upset and embarrassed to take up any more of her time."

Susie pushed back her chair and stood. "Now I need to go get Cammie and Matt. For their sakes, see if you can find the gumption to show up at the dinner table tonight. And for your sake, I'd suggest sleeping on the bedroom sofa tonight. I am not feeling at all kindly toward you, Ben Edmonds."

"That's fine. I'm not feeling too kindly toward myself."

The part of her that had always and would always love Ben wanted to go to him and hug him. But that part was no longer in charge. Anthill-loving Susie was, and she'd damn well had enough.

LATE OCTOBER in North Carolina could be chilly, but not as chilly as Ben's bedroom had been for the past two nights. Very early Wednesday morning—before the sun had even risen—Ben sat in his small office in the garage area at Double S Racing. He couldn't bear the silence that hung thick and heavy in the air when he and Susie were in the same room, and yet he didn't know how to fix it. Hell, he didn't know how to fix much of anything. Counting this coming weekend, there were four races left in the NASCAR Sprint Cup season and quite possibly four races left in his driving career.

The sole bright spot—at least it would have been bright if Ben could have worked up the energy to care—was that Hometeam Insurance had decided to sponsor Ben's car for another year. The personal approach had worked with them, at least, if not Susie. She didn't want to hear sorry, she'd said. She wanted to hear all the other words that went around that sorry. But Ben didn't have those words to give…not without saying a whole lot of other stuff he didn't want to get into with her. And so his marriage was becoming a reflection of his career—one guy going nowhere, fast.

Ben's cell phone, which was sitting on his otherwise cleared desk, began the ringtone he'd programmed in for Susie's calls. It was a spicy Latin song, full of sass, just as she was. At least, just as she was when she wasn't so ticked at him that she refused to speak altogether. He answered the phone, mainly to hear what the first nonessential words she had chosen to give him in nearly two days might be.

After they'd exchanged stilted hellos, she said, "I'd like to take you to lunch today since you're leaving for Talladega this evening. Do you have the time?"

"Yes," he replied. "Where should I meet you?"

"I'll be out running errands most of the day. I'll just pick you up at the garage around noon."

"Sounds good," he said, though *good* might have been an overstatement. And then he ended the call and got back to the business of going nowhere fast.

CHAPTER TEN

SINCE MURDER was out of the question, Susie had found herself a new felony and she liked it very, very much.

"You're smiling," Ben commented from the passenger seat of the family SUV.

"I might be," she replied.

"I've missed your smile."

Not nearly as much as I've missed yours.

They had left the garage minutes before and now were in downtown Mooresville. Susie quickly glanced into the front window of the Cut 'N' Chat as they passed by. Rue, her bright red hair as distinctive as her personality, was working on a customer. Rue would be proud of what Susie was about to do. Actually, all the Tarts would be.

"Hey, you missed an open spot," Ben said as they passed by Maudie's.

"An open spot for what?"

"To park. We're eating at Maudie's, right?"

"Not this time," she replied. "I have something a little different in mind."

"Okay," he said. "But not sushi or something equally off my food list, right?"

"No sushi," she agreed, still following the road out of town and into the countryside beyond. "We're having a picnic, just like we used to back before we could afford to eat out."

She slowed and made a right turn in to the county park that had been their personal playground back before Cammie and Matt had been born.

"I remember this place," Ben said.

"You should," Susie replied. "We used to come here about once a month."

He nodded. "Our dinner date."

The park was no big deal…just a stretch of lightly wooded land with a small pond at the far end. Few people used it, and that had been one of its charms. They had pretended that it was their private spot, back before they'd had land of their own. Susie had checked it out yesterday as her plan had been forming; the place was little changed in the years since she'd last been here. Susie parked in the five-space asphalt lot by the pond. They were the sole visitors, which was a blessing.

"Would you mind getting the picnic basket out of the cargo area?" Susie asked Ben once they'd exited the SUV.

"No problem," he replied as he walked to the rear of the vehicle.

Heart slamming in her chest, Susie headed down the gentle, grassy incline to the pond.

"Uh, honey? Could you hit the Unlock button on the key fob?" Ben called.

"Sure," Susie replied. She couldn't believe she was going to do this, but if she didn't, she had no one to blame but herself for her troubles with Ben. She took a deep breath and screwed up her courage.

Three…

Two…
One…
Done.

BEN HAD JUST PULLED OUT the big wicker picnic hamper when he heard the jingle of keys followed by a splashing sound.

"Hey, was that a fish?" he called to Susie, not quite able to make sense of what he'd heard.

"It wasn't a fish," she replied. "It was our keys."

Ben set down the basket. He'd been driving long enough that the track noise had made his hearing admittedly less than perfect.

"What did you say?"

"I said it was our keys."

Ben rounded the SUV to find Susie standing about five feet back from the pond's edge, looking calm and cool. Something still wasn't computing for him.

"You dropped the keys into the water? We'll probably need a new fob, but it's no big deal."

"I didn't drop them, I threw them," she said in a sugar sweet voice.

"You *what?*"

He ran down to the water, which even this late in the year was a rich algae-green. He could see no more than a few inches down. Not willing to give up on the keys, he edged even closer to the pond's margin, his shoes sinking in the wet earth.

"Don't ruin your shoes," his obviously crazy wife replied. "The keys are way out there."

He turned to stare at her, and she nodded in affirmation.

"I have a good arm," she said. "It's all the cleaning

up after the kids, I think. And you wouldn't believe how much Cammie's tack trunk weighs."

"Forget Cammie's tack trunk. Why the hell would you do this?" he asked as he stalked back up the hill, to where she'd retreated.

"To kidnap you, of course."

Ben snorted. "Right. Of course."

"I'm not joking. You're not leaving here until you've talked to me, and I mean *really* talked to me, about what's the matter with you."

"What's the matter with me? What about *you?* Are you out of your mind?" He reached into his pocket for his cell phone and then scrolled through his contact list, trying to decide who would be the best person to come get him and also not spread the tale.

"Don't bother," Susie said.

"What do you mean, don't bother? I'm not talking to you right now. You have clearly lost your grip on reality."

"Oh, I'd say I'm still pretty sharp. Sharp enough that I called in your phone as lost a couple of hours ago and asked them to cut service to it. Go through that list until your finger is callused, but no one is going to be here to pick you up until I decide it's time." She waggled her cell phone at him, then said, "I still have service," as she tucked it into her jeans pocket.

Ben stalked back to the SUV and circled it while letting go of a few words that could melt paint.

"Feel better now?" Susie asked when he'd finally given up any idea of hot-wiring his own vehicle.

"Not by a long shot."

"Then let's get through this. Why didn't you want to go see Adriana with me? What's the big problem with taking a few hours out of your moody self-reflection to think about someone else? I know you're having career troubles, but it's not always about you. We're a family, Ben, and this time it was about me. All I wanted was for you to be there and be a part of what I'm doing. It's our savings and I know I have the right to take some—"

Something inside Ben snapped. A few minutes ago, he'd been able to see some small shimmer of humor in this situation. Now it was gone…as dried up as his money flow was going to be.

"There is no money to invest in your business," he shouted. "How naive can you be, Susie? Do you have no idea how bad the markets have been? Hell, do you have any idea what it costs a month to keep this family's lifestyle afloat? There is no extra money. None! And you should have known this!"

It was almost an out-of-body experience. From some-place far away, he could see the angry man pacing back and forth. He could hear the words that just kept coming and coming, and it couldn't really be from him.

"Do you know what it's like to be me?" the angry man shouted. "Do you know how damn hard I work and how damn scared I am to see it all slipping away? No! You just take Cammie to ride that horse of hers that costs more to board and feed in a month than most families are lucky to see. You sign Matt up for more travel teams, plan more vacations, and all along, I'm drowning! You have no stinking idea how messed up my life is!"

And then from that place far away, Ben saw Susie. Pale, shocked Susie. The woman he'd sworn to love and cherish until he'd drawn his last breath, and instead he was frightening her. The fury burned out as quickly as it had arrived, leaving Ben back in his body and cold ashes in his mouth. He turned away and wiped at the moisture in his eyes, then turned back to face the damage he'd done, and not just from today.

"Susie? Honey?"

She continued to gaze out over the water.

"I always loved this place," she said.

He went to her and wrapped his arms around her. She stood unmoving and unwilling in his embrace.

"I'm so, *so* sorry," he said. "You're the one person I've always had to turn to, and instead I've been cutting you out."

She relaxed into him a little, and he knew that all was not lost. Of course, how could it be with Susie? She gave more than any woman he'd ever known.

"I'm an idiot," he said. "I just realized that I've been angry with you for not knowing things I've refused to discuss with you, and that's just flat out crazy."

She settled the side of her face against his chest in just the spot she did when they used to slow dance like teenagers to the sound of their car radio at this very pond.

"As crazy as kidnapping you?" she asked.

"Crazier. Way crazier." Ben made a little space between them and then with the backs of his fingers under her chin, gently urged her face up so that her gaze would meet his. "Let's go sit on the picnic table, okay?"

That had been their talking spot, back then.

"I didn't want to go to Adriana's because I knew you were going to hear things I'd been trying to protect you from. We're not starving, but we don't have the kind of cash that we did a few years ago, and that makes me feel like I've failed you. I figured I had enough years left as a driver that between the market rebounding and my endorsement deals, I could bail us back out and you'd never have to know or worry."

"I don't need protection, Ben. I'm pretty tough in my own way, and I'm pretty aware, too. I read the news, but honestly, you'd pretty much have to have been living in a cave these past few years not to know that everyone has taken a financial hit. I figured we weren't immune. If I need to borrow to expand my business, I will."

"You don't have to," Ben said. "I just had too much coming at me at the same time to react well. We have the money, and we'll use it for your business."

"We can pare back, too. The kids and I know that the horse and the travel teams and all those other things we've fallen into doing are luxuries. No one is going to perish if they're gone. At the end of the day, what's important is each of us…all of us…together as a family."

He reached over and settled one hand on hers, where they rested on her bent knees.

"I know. I just haven't been thinking too clearly. Things have become…complicated." He drew a breath and then let it slowly ease out. "As long as we're getting everything into the open, you need to know there's a chance I could lose my ride with Double S. Not as big a chance as a week ago, before Hometeam agreed to be my major sponsor again next season, but still a chance. It's not as though I'm a consistent performer anymore," he added in what he considered a colossal piece of understatement.

"How do you feel about that?" she asked.

He considered how he felt at this moment, since everything before this new clarity had settled on him was of no import.

"A little scared," he said. "But also kind of at peace with the fact that sooner or later, this is going to happen. And I guess if it does happen, I might be a little relieved, too."

"Relieved?" she echoed.

"Huh. Yeah, I guess so. I didn't know it until the word slipped out, but I'm tired of not having any fun. As the kids say these days, it has been one fun suck of a season."

"No fun?" She gave him a mock stern look. "Ben Edmonds, what's the Edmonds family rule?"

"Have fun," he automatically replied.

"That's right. Have fun. And if it's no longer fun, Ben, stop. Please. I promise we'll all be okay."

Stop. That was where the fear came in.

"If I stop, what will I do?"

"Whatever you want to," Susie replied. "If you still want a job in the NASCAR world, you'll have one. You're smart and well-respected. Whether you work with a supplier or go into management, you know there's a home for you. So the question is, what do you want?"

"I guess I want to find the fun again, then go out on my terms." He shook his head when another thought occurred. "It's kind of sad the way I've been riding Chris Sampson to talk to me, when I've been avoiding the same thing with you."

"You know, it's possible he's scared, too," Susie said. "Take it from me, it's just as tough to step into a new venture as it is to step out of an old one. Put yourself in his shoes. This is his first season as a crew chief and he's been paired with a grizzled old veteran."

Ben laughed. "Grizzled?"

She ran her hand along his jaw. "A little, but I like it."

"Good thing," he replied. "Because you're stuck with me."

"And thankful for it."

"I think you're right about Chris," he said. "I think he's just been trying too hard to establish himself as part of the team."

"I guess you should have talked to me sooner, eh?" she asked in a teasing voice.

"I guess I never should have stopped," he said, then hauled her onto his lap. "And I never will again. And I won't stop doing this, either." Ben let word follow deed and kissed his wife. "I hope you'll forgive me."

She shifted in his lap as she reached into her pocket.

"I forgive you enough to give you…*these!*"

She waggled the keys to the SUV in front of them.

Ben tipped back his head and laughed.

"And so the splash I heard?" he asked when he was done.

"Just some old keys from the kitchen junk drawer," she replied. "I might be crazy, but I'm not *that* crazy."

But Ben was. He was crazy in love with his talented, aggravating and perfectly wonderful wife.

EPILOGUE

Second place!

Second freaking place!

Ben couldn't stop smiling. From start to finish, the Talladega race had been magic. And when the magic returned, so did the reporters…in droves. He had barely cleared the pit area before being surrounded.

"So, Ben, from forty-first to second in a week. What do you attribute the turnaround to?" asked one microphone wielding woman.

He attributed it to Susie. It had been all Susie and the Edmonds family rule. He knew that she'd been glued to the television the whole race; he'd felt her love and support even though she was hundreds of miles away. And he needed to thank her now.

"Hang on," he said to the reporter. "First things, first."

He looked for his crew chief and spotted him about ten feet to his left. They'd had one helluva talk late into Wednesday night; there would be no more turf wars. In fact, there might even be the start of a friendship.

"Hey, Chris, toss me your phone," he said. "I need to call my wife."

"Sure thing," Chris replied, and then reached into his pocket.

The phone flew to Ben in a perfect arc, and his hand closed around it in a sure grip. The fun was back, and for as long as it was here, Ben would let it roll.

* * * * *

Love Inspired™®

Bestselling author

JILLIAN HART

brings readers another heartwarming story
from

the
GRANGER FAMILY RANCH

To fulfill a sick boy's wish, rodeo star Tucker Granger surprises
little Owen in the hospital. And no one is more surprised than
single mother Sierra Baker. But somehow Tucker ropes her heart
and fills it with hope. Hope that this country girl and her son
can lasso the roaming bronc rider into their family forever.

Look for

His Country Girl

*Available January
wherever books are sold.*

www.SteepleHill.com

Steeple
Hill®

LI87643

Stay up-to-date on all your romance-reading news with the brand-new Harlequin *Inside Romance!*

The Harlequin *Inside Romance* is a **FREE** quarterly newsletter highlighting our upcoming series releases and promotions!

Click on the *Inside Romance* link on the front page of **www.eHarlequin.com** or e-mail us at InsideRomance@Harlequin.ca to sign up to receive your **FREE** newsletter today!

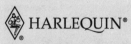

C.C. COBURN
Colorado Cowboy

American Romance's
Men of the West

It had been fifteen years since Luke O'Malley,
divorced father of three, last saw his high school
sweetheart, Megan Montgomery. Luke is shocked to
discover they have a son, Cody, a rebellious teen on his
way to juvenile detention. The last thing either of them
expected was nuptials. Will these strangers rekindle
their love or is the past too far behind them?

**Available January
wherever books are sold.**

"LOVE, HOME & HAPPINESS"

har75341

MARGARET WAY

Wealthy Australian,
Secret Son

Rohan was Charlotte's shining white knight
until he disappeared—before she had
the chance to tell him she was pregnant.

But when Rohan returns years later as
a self-made millionaire, could the blond,
blue-eyed little boy and Charlotte's heart
keep him from leaving again?

Available January 2011

REQUEST YOUR FREE BOOKS!

2 FREE NOVELS PLUS 2 FREE GIFTS!

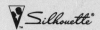

SPECIAL EDITION

Life, Love and Family!

SSE10R